D0733664

Blaze

Dear Reader,

I was born in Texas and have lived here most of my life. And I love it. Living in Texas is like living in a small country. Driving north from the Mexico border at Brownsville to Texhoma in the panhandle takes fifteen hours. Driving east from the New Mexico border at El Paso to Louisiana takes twelve.

On the Gulf Coast where I live, humidity reigns, but in far west Texas's Big Bend, the weather can be bone-dry. I live at 141 feet above sea level, but in the Davis and Guadalupe mountain ranges, peaks reach as high as 8,700 feet. Every comfort I might want I can find within ten minutes. In west Texas, I can drive for miles and see nothing.

That's why I chose west Texas as the setting for *One Good Man*. It's big and wild and untamed. And it's the perfect setting for a good guy to get his girl— once he gets rid of the bad guy, of course. Such is the story of Texas Ranger Sergeant Kell Harding, and his girl, Jamie Danby, who's seen as much horror in her life as has her Ranger.

Visit me anytime at www.alisonkent.com, where you can read excerpts from all the novels I've written for Harlequin over the years.

All my best,

Alison Kent

Alison Kent

ONE GOOD MAN

HARLEQUIN®

TORONTO • NEW YORK • LONDON
AMSTERDAM • PARIS • SYDNEY • HAMBURG
STOCKHOLM • ATHENS • TOKYO • MILAN • MADRID
PRAGUE • WARSAW • BUDAPEST • AUCKLAND

Recycling programs
for this product may
not exist in your area.

ISBN-13: 978-0-373-79498-0

ONE GOOD MAN

Copyright © 2009 by Mica Stone.

www.eHarlequin.com

Printed in U.S.A.

ABOUT THE AUTHOR

Alison Kent is the author of five sexy books for Harlequin Temptation—including *Call Me*, which she sold live on CBS *48 Hours*—several steamy books for Harlequin Blaze, including Waldenbooks bestsellers *The Sweetest Taboo* and *Kiss & Makeup*, and a number of sizzling books for Kensington Brava, including the Smithson Group series, as well as a handful of fun and sassy stories for other imprints. She is also the author of *The Complete Idiot's Guide to Writing Erotic Romance*. Alison lives in a Houston, Texas, suburb, with her own romance hero.

Books by Alison Kent

To HK, WD, k2, JM and SF, who made me laugh at least once every day while writing this. And to Walt, who makes me laugh every day whether I'm writing or not. You, dear, are the best of all good men.

1

GRUDGINGLY ACCEPTING her repetitive routine as a sure sign of impending spinsterhood, Jamie Danby still began every day the same way—with a two-mile run, a shower and clothes change, then a large cup of coffee, a banana-bran muffin and the front page of the *Reeves County News*.

The paper and the breakfast she picked up each morning on her way to work. When weather permitted, she walked.

It was only six blocks from her two-bedroom cottage to the Cantu Corner Store—Dolores Cantu baked the muffins herself and saved the plumpest of the batch for Jamie—and only another ten to Weldon Pediatrics, the small West Texas practice where Jamie had worked as office manager for six years.

Because she walked, she usually finished her coffee before she arrived. Her mother knew this, being as familiar with Jamie's daily routine as with her own.

On those days, Dr. Kate, as she was fondly referred to by the county's residents, would bring Jamie a refill, picking it up with her own breakfast—an egg, potato, cheese and chorizo burrito, loaded and folded by

Dolores's husband, Juan—before making the drive five miles north to the Danby Veterinary Clinic.

This morning, Jamie was still outside the pediatrics office, a boxy building of brown siding with rock beds of succulents hugging the front, fitting her key into the door, when her mother's black Suburban pulled into the lot that would soon be teeming with bilingual mothers and children.

Jamie turned briefly, squinting against the sun as she watched Kate swing the SUV in a semicircle, the big vehicle's tires grinding on the gravel and creating a cloud of dust thick enough to gag a horse. Jamie's mother had always been more focused on her destination than the journey of getting there, and it showed in the way she drove.

Once the clinic's door was unlocked, Jamie dropped her keys into the bulky hobo bag hanging from her shoulder, and walked to where her mother waited. She took the coffee Kate handed her, removed the top from her empty cup, and settled the new one into the old.

After a quick sip, she smiled and said, "Where would I be without you to look after me?"

The corner of Kate's mouth, her lips smooth and free of added color, quirked to one side. "Married with children?"

It was an ongoing joke between overprotective mother and a daughter who had been through hell and only by a miracle survived. Though could Jamie really call it surviving?

Ten years later she was still in hiding, existing not as

her own woman, but as a creation of the horrific crime she'd witnessed when she'd been just nineteen years old.

Not having kids or a husband was, in her case, for the best. Should her memories of what she'd seen return, she didn't know if she'd be fit to live with, or if the remembered trauma would send her over the edge.

No, the future Jamie saw for herself was one spent alone. And, really—she was okay with it. Independence. Doing her own thing. A woman, an island unto herself. Seriously. How bad could spinsterhood be?

Another sip, and she thought back to what her mother had said. "I'm too spoiled for marriage and children. I like getting my own way all the time."

Kate shook her head, and reached for her own coffee where it steamed from the holder built into the Suburban's center console. "I'll cop to being a hovering nuisance, but the spoiling is your own doing. I was always too busy working and worrying to waste time seeing to your every whim."

Jamie nearly choked, but managed to swallow and come up laughing. "Are you kidding me? Where do you think I learned the art? You were the best teacher a girl could have." She raised her cardboard cup as proof. "You still are."

"Humph." Kate shook her head, fought a smile with a frown. "It would only be spoiling if I were stopping at the Cantus' just for you. But since I'm stopping for my own breakfast, it's not."

"You keep telling yourself that," Jamie said, lifting a hand to wave at Roni and Honoria, two of her coworkers who carpooled to Weldon from Alpine, and had just arrived in Honoria's sedan. "And I'll keep enjoying being single and an only child."

Kate arched a brow, studying her daughter's face as if the right angle might show her something new. "Sounds to me like you learned more from me than spoiling. You learned the art of self-deception as well."

Jamie tilted her cup against her mother's in a toast. They were two of a kind, gracefully accepting what life had served them. And though both would rather things had turned out differently, neither would give up the bond they now shared to make it so. "You have a busy day ahead of you?"

Kate nodded, pushing up the brim of the Danby Veterinary ball cap that covered the short wedge of her silvered brown hair. "The Barneses are bringing in their litter of shepherd pups. Two spays and six neuters."

"Which means you'd better get going."

"Which means I'd better get going. Besides—" Kate angled her chin in the direction of the clinic "—it looks like your staff has something on their mind."

Jamie followed the direction of her mother's gaze. Just inside the plate-glass entrance, Roni and Honoria stood facing each other, gesturing dramatically in Jamie's direction. She couldn't imagine what had them so animated this early. The day's first patient had yet to arrive.

She backed away from her mother's Suburban and hefted her bag more securely over her shoulder. "I'd better see what's going on. And you've got a dozen testicles calling your name. Thanks for the refill."

As her mother pulled out of the parking lot, leaving with a full-arm wave, Jamie headed for the front door.

She opened it to the sound of scurrying feet squeaking on the tiled floor as Honoria disappeared down the hallway toward the examination rooms.

Roni had obviously been in a similar hurry to take her seat at the front desk. Her headset was on crooked, and as Jamie came closer, she saw an insurance file open in front of the other woman. A tall blonde Laurel to Honoria's short dark Hardy, Roni stared at her computer monitor, doing her comical best to pretend she was hard at work.

Jamie blew the other woman's cover by reaching across the reception counter and turning the file right side up. "Might as well spill it now before the two of you explode. With Dr. Griñon here only half a day, I won't have time to clean up the mess if you do."

"Why are his half days the busiest of the week? And why don't we get to leave at noon, too?" Roni asked, forcing a light laugh as she situated the folder to her liking. She refused to meet Jamie's gaze. "I swear, Wednesdays should be relaxing, but they can really suck."

They could, but Jamie knew when Roni was grabbing for a distraction. The spots of color high on her cheeks told the tale. "You're changing the subject."

"Am I?" The color brightened. "I thought I was commenting on what you just said. You know, making conversation?"

"I'm not going away, so you might as well fess up." Jamie set her bag and her breakfast on the counter that rose in front of the desk, and her gaze on Roni, snapped open the single-section newspaper.

No sooner had she smoothed it out than Roni grabbed

it, hiding it beneath the desk in her lap, ignoring the "gimme" motion Jamie made with her hand. "Honoria said she wanted to talk to you first thing."

"What about?" And more importantly, how much of Jamie's paper was salvageable, and how much was smeared on Roni's pink scrub pants?

"I don't know, I mean, I don't remember." Flustered, Roni stood and leaned across the counter to call out, "Honoria! Jamie's here!"

As if Roni's partner in crime wasn't already aware. Jamie sighed. "This better not be some early surprise birthday-party thing…" Surely her mother would still be outside if it was, ready to come in and sing and blow noisemakers with the other two.

Roni met Jamie's gaze, frowning for a moment before her brown doe eyes went wide. "If there's a surprise party, I don't know anything about it, and this isn't it. Honoria! Get your butt out here now!"

Jamie sighed. Dear Roni, giving it away without admitting to a thing. Jamie's birthday wasn't for another two weeks, but she knew no one was going to let the momentous occasion of her turning thirty come and go quietly. That's how it was for old maids.

Honoria emerged from the file room, the morning's patient charts clutched to her ample chest. *Ample* was Jamie's word. Honoria considered herself short and dumpy and copy-paper plain—but then she'd never seen herself light up like the desert sky when her husband, Vicente, swept her away from the clinic for a private lunch.

Right now, the only thing bright about her were her eyes as her gaze bore into Roni's, broadcasting her disbelief that the blonde couldn't handle things on her own. Obviously, the two hadn't had time to get their story straight.

Whatever they were up to, it would have to wait. Jamie was hungry. "I'm going to the break room to eat my breakfast and read whatever part of the paper I can. Come get me when you've figured out how to tell me whatever it is you don't want me to know."

She lifted her bag by the shoulder strap, grabbed her coffee with the same hand, and reached with the other for the newspaper Roni still held captive.

Roni, having sat again, remained as silent and smiling as long-faced Laurel. Jamie turned to the Hardy of the duo. "I need my morning news. You know how I am without my morning news."

Honoria nodded, not a strand of her short wavy hair moving. Neither did her lips, not right away, and her eyes had gone flat. For the first time since walking into the comedy routine, Jamie was not amused. "What's going on, guys?"

"You don't want to see the newspaper today, *mija*." Honoria pulled a copy of the latest *O Magazine* from her stack of files. She worshipped Oprah like she would a goddess. "Read Oprah instead. She has good, positive, cheery things to say."

Meaning whatever was in the *Reeves County News* was a bad, negative downer. Jamie thought quickly. Her mother was fine. She had yet to see Dr. Griñon today, but if something had happened to the clinic's pediatrician, Laurel and Hardy here wouldn't be hiding it. And they were both here, so there was nothing going on with their families.

Families. Jamie's father. He hadn't been a part of her life for ten years. Not since she'd been nineteen, attending Texas Tech University at Junction, living with her parents on their struggling ranch between Junction and Sonora, and working on Interstate 10 as a waitress at the Sonora Nites Diner. It had been his choice to walk out of her life, to leave her and her mother to deal with the things he hadn't been strong enough to handle. That didn't mean bad news wouldn't hurt.

"Is it my dad?" She knew it wasn't. Her mother would have told her had something happened to Steven Monroe. Which left only…that other thing.

Once more, Jamie set down her belongings and waited for the paper. This time, she wasn't taking no for an answer. Sharing a sad look with Honoria, Roni placed the folded and wrinkled sheets into Jamie's shaking hand.

There was only one thing that could have happened. Only one thing her friends would keep from her. Not because they didn't want her to know—she would find out eventually no matter what—but because of the wounds the news would reopen.

What her friends didn't understand was that the wounds had never really closed.

She crushed the paper, looked from Roni to Honoria, tears filling her eyes and blurring her vision, emotion lodged in her throat like a red rubber ball. "They found the last body, didn't they?"

Both pairs of brown eyes held distress and sympathy and fear. Jamie felt only one of the three. Her hands continued to tremble, her stomach twisted and gripped. Her friends nodded, first one, then the other, tears rolling down Honoria's cheeks as Roni choked back a sob.

Neither woman had known Jamie at the time of the murders—she and her mother had moved to Weldon not long after—and no one other than Jamie's parents and the authorities involved knew the details of that night.

Not even the families of the other victims—the victims who had died, and the one who had been dragged from the diner against his will. Jamie had been a victim, too, but that fact seemed lost on those left behind.

They'd demanded answers, had called her a liar, a coward, when the truth was she'd had no answers to give. She knew their lashing out was a coping mechanism; it gave them something to do when they felt so helpless. They wanted to know why she had been the one to live instead of their children, their siblings, their spouse. But most of all they wanted to know why she couldn't remember enough of that night to help authorities catch the person who'd destroyed so many lives.

She breathed deeply, tasted bile at the back of her throat and spread the newspaper open to the headline on the front page.

FIFTH VICTIM OF SONORA NITES DINER MURDERS IDENTIFIED

Remains discovered in the Davis Mountains State Park this past March have, through dental records, been positively identified as belonging to Kass Duren, the hostage taken at gunpoint from the Sonora Nites Diner ten years ago following the after-hours robbery and shooting spree that left all but one employee dead.

Jamie had been that one employee. She stopped reading and thought back, trying to remember what she'd heard about the discovery of a body. Nothing came to mind. Either she'd blocked it out, or she'd read nothing about the find. The former seemed likely, but still…

Kass Duren. The cook. His wife's name was Helen. He'd been what he'd called peasant stock. Sturdy and solid. Descended from potato farmers from the old country. Jamie, at nineteen, had never asked which one.

"I remember so little about it." Her voice came out soft, words she heard in her mind more than with her ears. "Colors, sounds. Flashes of light. It's all one big mess. Like sharp bursts or abstract pieces." She closed her eyes, felt the tingle of perspiration bite at her skin. "They had to tell me that Kass had been taken away."

She looked back at her closest friends, the only two people with whom she had trusted her story when she could no longer hold it in, knowing they would never betray her, or reveal the truth of her past. Both were silent, pale. And when her cell phone played like a country-western band in her bag, they both jumped along with her. She dug it out, glancing at the number on the screen.

"I'm fine," she told her mother without waiting for Kate to speak. "Go to work. There's nothing you can do here."

"Jamie. I'm so sorry."

Jamie found herself shaking her head. "Don't be. Kass's wife needs this closure. It's taken way too long."

"I know, sweetie, but there's going to be so much press, and so many reporters digging into that night. You've been safe here. Goddammit." There was a pause while Kate made a turn; Jamie heard the signal click on and off. "I should've moved you across the country, or at least across the state."

"We're in Texas, Mom. Half the state *is* almost half the country." Jamie forced a laugh, hoping it sounded better on the other end of the call because she was not buying the humor here.

"We need to talk about this. If your name shows up in the paper…"

Panicked, Jamie stopped listening. She hadn't read the whole article, and skimmed it quickly, finding no mention of who she was now, or who she'd been then. "It's not there. My name's not there."

"Not in this article, no, but what about the next, because you know this will renew interest in the case. They'll reopen the investigation. They'll figure out that Stephanie Monroe fell off the face of the earth and go looking. And someone with the right connections, or a big-enough gun, can find out that Dr. Kate Danby used to be Dr. Ruth Monroe."

Another pause and her mother was talking again. "I'm coming back. We need to talk to the authorities. And how the hell did the news make it into the paper without someone in law enforcement giving us a call?"

At the sound of the clinic door opening, Jamie turned, one arm hugged tightly around her middle that was roiling and surging in advance of the oncoming tidal wave she feared would sweep her away. "Oh my God."

"What is it? Jamie? What's happening?"

"They're calling now, Mom. In person," she added as the door swooshed closed, leaving Jamie face-to-face with the long arm of the law.

2

A SERGEANT with Company E in Midland, and assigned to the Unsolved Crimes Investigation Team, Texas Ranger Kellen Harding felt like a bull inside the china shop of Weldon Pediatrics—though the way the three women in front of him were staring, he might be well on his way to becoming a steer.

"I'll have to call you back, Mom," said the one Kell had already pegged as Jamie Danby, the one who had lived the first nineteen years of her life as Stephanie Monroe. The Hispanic woman was too short and, well, Hispanic. The blonde was the right height, and hair was easily colored, but she didn't have the same snap as the brunette—the brunette who was giving him a hell of an evil eye.

He stayed where he was, just inside the door, removed his white Stetson and sunglasses, and held her gaze. "Jamie Danby?"

Her face blanched, but color quickly returned to her cheekbones, and her mouth barely trembled when she asked, "And you are?"

"Ranger Sergeant Kellen Harding, ma'am, of Unsolved Crimes." He added the extra to break the ice that was taking too long to thaw. It was time he didn't want to waste, and she might not have.

"Can we help you with something, Sergeant Harding?" She faced him squarely, her chin up, her gaze direct. She didn't even bother looking around for a sick child. She knew he was here for her, and because of the recent break in the Sonora Nites Diner case.

He wondered if she was aware of the crumpled newspaper she held. He gave a nod toward it. "You've seen the story?"

"Of Kass being found?" she asked, her hand tightening around the strap of her bag, her knuckles turning white.

It was a rhetorical question, but it answered his, and he nodded again just the same. "Is there somewhere we can talk? Privately?"

"You can use the break room," the blonde hurried to offer, straightening the headset slipping down one side of her neck.

"Or there's a table and chairs on the back patio," the Hispanic woman added, a stack of folders in her arms. "It's a covered patio. With a ceiling fan."

Kell looked at Jamie. Jamie looked at Kell. It was her call, but he had a feeling no place on the clinic grounds would qualify as private. To tell the truth, he mused as the air-conditioning kicked on and the building's windows rattled, he had a feeling no place in Weldon would.

That was the thing about small towns. Folks liked to keep up with their neighbors' business, even when that business was none of their concern. Since authorities had never had a suspect to arrest and bring to trial for the murders, witness protection hadn't been an option for Stephanie Monroe. Her mother Ruth, now Kate Danby, had taken matters into her own hands, choosing to protect her daughter by changing their names and hiding in plain sight.

If anyone came after Jamie, the whole town would be waiting. Weldon's eleven hundred residents didn't need the details of her past spelled out before they'd come to her aid; she was one of their own and nothing else mattered—a fact Kell was sure Kate had counted on.

As plans went, it wasn't a bad one, but Kell liked his better. He was here to put an end to any and all threats this case still posed to her as the only witness to the Sonora Nites Diner murders. He just needed Jamie to hear him out, and then to go along with his proposal. Now that he saw her as more than a name in a file, he figured he was in for a fight. She might be rattled, but she was not down for the count.

Without looking toward them, Jamie spoke to the women standing behind her. "Can you two manage the patients and the doctor and the phones for a while?"

At her question, they both nodded, the blonde adding, "They invented voice mail for a reason, Jamie. We'll be fine. Go."

"And don't worry if you can't get back. It's a short appointment day anyway. We can handle the afternoon on our own." This from the darker woman.

Jamie took them at their word, folding the newspaper into her purse hanging from her shoulder, then reaching for her coffee and what Kell assumed was her breakfast in a brown paper bag.

He followed as she headed for the front door, catching it once she'd shoved at the glass, and returning his hat to his head, his sunglasses to his face, as he stepped onto the front walk behind her.

She held up one hand to shade her eyes, looking first at his four-wheel-drive SUV, then off down the block. "Can you leave your truck here? And take a walk?"

He could. "How far?"

"The Cantus have a covered deck with picnic tables at their market. Have you had breakfast? Juan makes awesome burritos."

Kell had poured himself a cup of coffee for the road when he'd left Midland before dawn, but that was it. "A burrito sounds great."

Jamie set off toward the sidewalk. Kell fell into step at her side. He was six foot one; he judged her to be about five foot eight and a whole lot of that height to be leg. She matched him step for step as they silently hit the end of one block and crossed the street to the next.

From behind the sunglasses he wore, he studied her. Her determination—she never faltered. Her focus—she trained it ahead, but that didn't keep her from paying attention to movement on all sides.

She was sharp, aware. She wasn't going to fall apart at the first sign of trouble. No, if Kell was going to have trouble with this case, it would no doubt have to do with the way she filled out the flower-pink bottoms of her scrubs.

He'd always been an ass man, and he'd never seen a tighter one than Jamie Danby's. Combine that with the rest of what she had going for her, and it was going to take a whole lot of discipline to keep his eye on the prize.

He pulled his lingering gaze away, catching the quirk of her mouth as they crossed one last intersection into the parking lot of the Cantu Corner Store. She didn't admit to knowing he'd had his eye on her backside, but then she didn't have to. That wicked half grin was her tell.

They stepped up onto the raised cedar deck; he let her take the lead and choose the table farthest from both the store and the street. She left her coffee and her bag behind and went inside. Again, that kind of town. One where she didn't have to worry about purse snatchers or identity theft.

Instead, she had to worry about a killer following the media coverage of his handiwork discovering who and where she was and hunting her down.

While Jamie heated what turned out to be a muffin in the small store's community microwave, Kell ordered two breakfast burritos and doctored a large coffee as they were being made. Once he and Jamie were back outside and settled at their table—and out of earshot of the curious onlookers inside the store—Jamie pounced.

"You're here because finding Kass's body reminded you that there's still a killer out there. Is that right?"

Kell stopped with his first burrito halfway to his mouth. "I've never forgotten there's a killer out there. Not once in ten years."

She met his gaze, hers not so much disbelieving as challenging. He knew it would take more than words to dispel her feelings that she'd been alone all this time, on her own, abandoned.

"You know I don't remember anything about the killer, so whatever you're hoping to find out, you can stop." She broke her muffin in half. Wisps of banana-scented steam rose, and she broke one of the halves again. "There's nothing there. My noggin broke. It didn't retain a thing about what he looked like, what he wore, nothing. You may have found Kass and solved the mystery of what happened to him, but the mystery of who's responsible remains." She paused, frowned, stared at the chunk of muffin she was ready to eat. "Unless that's why you're here. To tell me you have a suspect. To *warn* me you have a suspect, and that he knows where I am."

"No suspect," he said to set her at ease, biting off a quarter of his burrito while she calmed enough to eat the mangled muffin square. But she was wrong.

Just because she didn't remember anything about the killer didn't mean her noggin had broken, or that nothing was there. It *was* there. That much he knew, just as he knew it was hiding. He'd come here to get inside her head and coax it out.

She nodded thoughtfully as she ate, and he figured it was best to let her stew while he filled the hungry hole in his stomach. He was happy to answer any and all of her questions before getting to the reason he was here. But since he'd shown up unannounced, he didn't imagine she had many ready and waiting on the tip of her tongue.

She surprised him by having one, and with the way she took him in, her gaze causing the hair at his nape to stir. "Why did no one let us know about the identification before it hit the papers? Did you people lose the list of contact numbers you've had for us all these years?"

He'd only been assigned the case after the ID had been made and the files had been transferred from storage to the UCIT. The case was one he'd been aware of at the time of the killings, but he'd been in training academy then, and not yet a state trooper, much less the Ranger he was now.

Until the UCIT had been put in charge, he'd had no authority over how things were handled. He did now, and she was right. Jamie and her mother should have been informed.

He pulled his BlackBerry from its holster at his waist, punched up her contact information and showed her the screen. "I have all of your numbers. You're in the loop from here on. I promise."

He hadn't really answered her question, only guaranteed a similar lapse wouldn't happen on his watch. Whether or not that satisfied her, he couldn't say. She'd dropped her gaze and was back to picking at her muffin. It was hard not to watch her fingers at work, so precise, so nimble. So sure. "If you'd like to eat something besides crumbs, I'm happy to buy another round of burritos."

She shook her head, her eyes coming up, searching, soft, a little bit sad. "Go ahead if you want. I don't have much of an appetite."

He breathed deeply, hurting because she did. "Another coffee then?"

"No thanks." She pressed her fist to her sternum. "I think all that acid and caffeine was a mistake. It's going to take an Alka-Seltzer or Tums to get me through the rest of the morning."

Kell was pretty sure any stomach issues she was

having had less to do with what she'd put in it than with what she'd had to swallow when she'd seen the paper's front page. His showing up couldn't have made the news go down any easier. And what had he done since but make everything worse.

He got up from the table, and returned to the store to refill his own coffee and get Jamie a roll of antacids. Seeing a stack of *Reeves County News* copies in a rack next to the door helped him decide how to resume the conversation.

Once outside, he handed her the Tums and settled across the table from her again, folding his sunglasses into his shirt pocket before asking, "What's the first thing that went through your mind when you saw the headline?"

She peeled back the paper from the end of the roll. "There wasn't a first thing. It was more like a tumble of one thing on top of another."

Kell was good with going slowly, taking his time. "Such as?"

"That Roni's and Honoria's behavior made sense. They'd been going through all sorts of machinations to keep me from reading the news."

Roni would be the blonde, Honoria the Hispanic woman. Jamie had obviously shared some of her background with them. He made a mental note to add the info to his phone before prodding again. "What else?"

"That I needed to call my mother. That it wasn't going to be long before the media figured out Jamie Danby used to be Stephanie Monroe. This is the first movement the case has seen since it went cold, and investigative reporters these days are able to ferret out just about anything they want to know."

She shrugged, thumbed one of the tablets free and put it in her mouth, her fingers worrying the roll the only indication that her nerves weren't as calm as her voice. "My mother is the one who changed our identities. Once she realized we were on our own, she packed us up, sold the few head of livestock still on the ranch, filed for divorce, and we vanished. But her resources were way more limited than those available to whatever government agency handles witness protection. So I figure if reporters can find me after this break in the case, then the killer can, too.

"Except…" She paused, frowning as she gouged a thumbnail into the paper between the antacid tablets. "I've always assumed he knows. That he's left me alone because my amnesia means I'm not really a threat. That coming after me when it's clear he's gotten away with murder would be the stupidest move he could make."

The stupid ones didn't stand a chance. The smart ones, well, they could take longer to track down and bring to justice. But Kell *would* bring this one to justice. Jamie's family, Kass's family, the families of the other victims— they weren't the only ones who had suffered because of the killer who'd rampaged through the Sonora Nites Diner.

There was another man, the man who had taught Kell what it meant to be a Texas Ranger, who had lived and breathed the investigation, who had wept at every brick wall. As much as Kell was here for Jamie and Kate Danby, he was here for the man who had sworn to see this case through to the end, but who'd been hit and killed by a drunk driver while pulling over another on a long solemn stretch of Interstate 10.

This was Kell's job to finish now.

"On the other hand," she continued, popping a second antacid before closing the bits of paper around the roll's open end and tucking it into a pocket of her purse. "How smart could he possibly be to have left the diner that night without making sure there was no one still alive?"

Kell returned his cup of coffee to the table, holding it in place between both of his hands. "You're the one who outsmarted him by playing dead. You saved your own life, Jamie."

"Too bad I couldn't do the same for anyone else."

Her voice was flat, almost unfeeling. It didn't break with sadness over the loss of life, or sting with survivor's guilt. Though she'd walked out of that diner covered in blood, she spoke of the experience as would an outsider.

Locking away her emotions with her memories was a coping mechanism. Kell reached for the key. "What if you could do something now? For those who are left?"

Her eyes snapped, her breathing quickened. He'd hit the nerve he'd hoped for. "I told you. I told the cops and shrinks who questioned me then. I told the counselors I saw for months after. I can see splatters of color, and fractals of light and shadows as he moved through the diner. But I don't remember him. The last thing I see clearly is parking in the lot behind the diner before work. I barely remember opening the door and going inside."

She had gone inside. She had punched the time clock at 5:52 p.m.—eight minutes before her shift began. She had completed her six hours and—this was where Kell's imagination kicked in—had been joking around, maybe blowing off steam with her coworkers when the killer had slammed through the front door and opened fire.

Behind the register, Jamie—she'd been Stephanie then—had fallen to the floor. The killer had kicked her body out of the way to get to the cash register. Her ribs had been bruised so badly, the impression of his shoe's heel was visible in the blues and purples marring her skin.

She hadn't even moved when the killer had dragged away her boss. When the authorities arrived, she'd been lying exactly where she'd fallen, covered in her own blood and that of the others, her wounds fortunately no threat to her life.

What the crime scene photos and mock-up staging revealed, however, was that Jamie's position had her facing the front windows and the parking lot. If she'd opened her eyes even once, she might have seen... something. Car color, make or model. Numbers on the license plate. Killer's clothing, height or build. Age or ethnicity.

She might not have seen anything, but there was a very good chance that she had—and that she knew she had. Not consciously; the Jamie she was now wouldn't know anything about it. That's why Kell needed to ask Stephanie.

But he had to tread carefully to get from here to there. "I know you don't remember. Your mind is doing what it's supposed to do."

She gave a sharp snort. "It's supposed to fritz out? Really?"

"Not fritz out. Protect you. Amnesia is a coping mechanism." Just like her sarcasm.

"So it's all there. I'm just not thinking hard enough, or trying often enough to find it? Is that what you're saying? Because if you've come all this way for that—"

He cut her off before her accusations grew more strident, and got in the way of her listening to him. "That's not what I'm saying. Not at all. The memories are there, yes. But thinking hard or trying often is not how you'll find them."

She didn't believe him; he knew she was humoring him at best. "And I suppose you have the magic touch to make that happen?"

"Not me," he said softly, "but I know who might."

She waited, silent, expectant, as if bracing against him throwing a bucket of cold water in her face.

He got it over with as quickly as he could. "I'd like you to see a forensic hypnotist."

3

HE WOULD LIKE. *He* would like. Well, she didn't give a rat's ass what he would like. He wasn't the one whose head would explode if those memories ever came back.

"I'm sorry. I'm not sure what to call you. Sergeant? Ranger? Trooper?"

"Call me Kell," he said with too much twinkle in his green eyes for the subject at hand.

Murder needed to be looked at with serious intent. And if he was hoping to soften her up, to win her to his side with that sparkle, well, it was time he had his hopes dashed.

She started to do just that, but was stopped by the squeal of tires as her mother's Suburban took the turn into the Cantus' at a speed that would have scared a stunt driver straight. Jamie flinched, bracing for the SUV to ram the front of the store.

But the vehicle skidded to a stop, fishtailing to the left and throwing gravel, causing the Texas Ranger to surge to his feet with a deep "Holy hell."

"It's my mother," Jamie told him, enjoying the way his eyes went wide as much as she appreciated the width of his shoulders beneath his sharp white shirt. He was, in a word, hot. Disturbingly so. Big and intoxicating and lusty. Okay, more than a word, she thought, and cleared her throat. "I forgot to call her back."

Kate jumped out of the cab and came at them, waving her arms and yelling the very same thing. "You were supposed to call me back. Jamie. What's going on?"

On her feet now, too, Jamie made the introductions. "Mom, this is Sergeant Kell Harding with the Texas Rangers. Kell, my mother, Kate Danby. Dr. Kate."

Jamie's mother looked at the man in the Western-cut dress shirt, white hat, boots and jeans, then turned an inquiring gaze back on her daughter to wait for more than an exchange of names—a gaze filled with as many fears as questions.

Her own heart aching over the worry her mother had suffered all these years, Jamie took her hand and pulled Kate to sit on the bench beside her. "Kell came the moment he was given the case files. He came in person. He wanted to make sure we were okay. To answer our questions."

Jamie turned then to look at Kell. He again sat on the other side of the table, but rather than sit directly across from either her or her mother, he had positioned himself in between, giving them equal consideration. She liked that as much as she liked the creases fanning out from the corners of his eyes. They seasoned him with wisdom, not age, and spoke of experience Jamie knew was needed.

His attention on Kate, Kell inclined his head. "Your daughter's right, Dr. Danby. Any questions you have, ask—"

Kate cut him off. "You being given the files—does

that mean the case has finally been brought out of cold storage to thaw? That maybe we can put an end to this once and for all? Or are we going to have to spend the rest of our lives the way we've spent the last ten, fearful and looking over our shoulders, searching for whatever it is that's spooked us?"

Kell didn't look away. He pressed his lips together, and Jamie watched the muscles in his neck tighten as his jaw held taut. Around his coffee cup, his hands also tightened. She heard the plastic squeak. But he kept his frustration in check. And she knew it was frustration, not anger, not insult, and frustration with the case, not with her mother's accusation that he wasn't doing his job.

Finally, he found his words and spoke. "What Jamie didn't mention is that I work with the UCIT, the Unsolved Crimes Investigation Team. Cold cases are what I do, where I pour one-hundred percent of my energies. Right now, this case, Jamie's case, is my top priority."

"But only because of Kass Duren. Not because of Jamie," Kate said, and Jamie stiffened.

"Mom—"

"No, it's okay. She's right. Anytime there's activity on a case, it gets moved to the top of the list. That doesn't mean without movement it lies dormant. We're always looking for a break, a lead, new clues and witnesses."

"Looking?" Kate asked, her mouth grim and turned down, her Danby Veterinary Clinic ball cap pulled low. "Or waiting for them to fall into your lap? Because I don't see how you can give one hundred percent to any single case when you've got dozens of others still unsolved and demanding your time."

"He didn't say he gave one hundred percent to any single case. He said he prioritized." Jamie didn't know why she was defending the Texas Ranger.

She should be siding with her mother. They were the ones living this hell, the ones forgotten by law enforcement and left to their own devices, starting over, creating new identities, protecting themselves however they could because if they didn't, who would?

She decided it was because of Kell that her loyalties were wobbling. His sincerity. The pit-bull determination that had brought him all this way. He could've written a letter. He could've picked up the phone. He hadn't done either one. He'd driven the three hours between his office and hers.

Since the initial investigators had packed up and moved on, he was the first officer from any law enforcement agency to involve himself with Jamie and her mother directly. Now that she'd had a few minutes to cool down, she wanted to hear what he had to say.

If she'd learned anything over the last ten years it was to keep her eyes, mind and ears open. She told herself that she owed him that much. She told herself, too, that it wasn't because of his eyes. Or his shoulders. Or the size of his hands.

The fan whirring overhead stirred the hot dry air into a semblance of a breeze, pushing loose strands of her hair into her face. She plucked them away, ignored the heat stirring low in her belly and said, "Sergeant Harding—Kell—was about to explain forensic hypnosis to me."

Kate squeezed Jamie's wrist. "What?"

"I'm pretty sure he wants to jog my memory."

"The same memory you've told everyone repeatedly is blank? Does no one believe you?" Kate shifted on the bench, closer to Jamie and away from Kell. "Or since they're at a loss to solve this thing, are they now putting the onus on you?"

Kell had been sitting silent all this time, absorbing the exchange between mother and daughter as if searching for the best tack to take, or as if waiting his turn because, law enforcement or not, he knew he was the outsider.

But Kate's accusation obviously riled him. His pulse throbbed in his temples, and he had barely swallowed the rest of his coffee before he crushed the cup.

"The onus is on us, Dr. Danby. On me. Completely. Coming to Jamie is not a shifting of responsibility—"

Her skin pale, Kate pulled her hand from Jamie's and waved it to cut him off. "Then why are you talking to my daughter about hypnosis? Why—"

"Let him talk, Mom. Please." Jamie so understood what her mother was feeling.

It had been Kate's job to protect her daughter, to see Jamie from traumatized teen to a woman standing on her own, recovered, able to view the past from the distance she'd come in ten years. And she'd done it alone, while building a new life as a divorcée, coping with all of it at once because she'd had no choice. As much as Jamie did not want to return her to where this whole nightmare had started...

She tamped down the fear rising in a dark cloud around her and turned her attention on Kell. "Let him talk."

His gaze captured hers, held, a potent thank-you for not writing off his proposal before he'd had a chance to explain. A brief nod, then he looked at her mother, as if her permission was as important to him as was Jamie's.

She liked that. Found she was liking many things about him when the only thing that mattered was whether or not he would be the one to put an end to her hell.

Kate hadn't objected, so Kell cleared his throat. "Before you arrived, I was explaining to Jamie that the memories she thinks she's lost, well, she hasn't. Not really. Selective amnesia is a coping mechanism—"

"Selective amnesia? Are you saying she's forgotten on purpose?"

He shook his head. "Her subconscious won't let her remember. Her mind is protecting her from reliving the trauma of that night's events."

"And yet knowing that, you want to hypnotize her and have her suffer them again?" Kate shook her head vehemently. "No. No. It's not going to happen. Absolutely not."

"Mom—"

"Jamie, no." Kate's voice grew shrill. "I won't let you go through that again. You can't—"

It was time for Jamie to take charge. "I can, but I haven't said that I will. I want to know more before I agree to going back there."

Kell's expression changed, growing accommodating, respectful yet urgent, as if he was at her disposal for any little thing. "What do you want to know?"

Jamie wasn't even sure where to begin. "What makes you think this will work? This forensic hypnosis?"

"I'm not sure that it will," he told her, and she appreciated his honesty. "You may not recall anything we can use in our investigation. On the other hand, you might remember the very thing we need to track down this bastard and put him behind bars."

"Such as?" Jamie couldn't help but fear, what was for her, the unknown.

Her mother spoke before Kell could answer. "A license-plate number? Isn't that what that bus driver in California remembered under hypnosis?"

"You're talking about Chowchilla," Kell said, and nodded.

"What's Chowchilla?" Jamie asked.

"A town in California," Kell explained. "In 1976, three men kidnapped a busload of students and their driver, and held them hostage in a moving van buried in a quarry. A ransom note was found in the house of the quarry's owner. His son and two others were eventually charged."

Bury? A van? For a kidnapping? In the movies, sure, but for real? "You're kidding," she said, and when he shook his head, asked, "Were they rescued?"

"They were," Kell answered. "They dug themselves out, but by then, the kidnappers were long gone. The driver eventually underwent forensic hypnosis to see if he could remember anything helpful."

Bizarre. "And it worked?"

"He remembered enough of a license-plate number on one of the vehicles involved, that authorities were able to track the men down through the registration, I think it was. Hypnosis was also used in Ted Bundy's case. In the Boston Strangler's. In Sam Sheppard's. His was made into a movie. *The Fugitive.*" Kell's expression fell into a goofy smile. "With Harrison Ford."

Kate had been listening, and asked, "Are the memories refreshed during hypnosis even admissible in court?"

"Not everywhere, no. In Texas, they are, but we use them in conjunction with other investigative tools."

Meaning a conviction or acquittal wouldn't rest solely on what Jamie might manage to recall. "So if I remember seeing a license plate through the diner's window…"

"Then we'll track down what car those plates were on at the time and who it was registered to."

And to play devil's advocate. "Someone other than the owner could've been driving it."

Kell nodded. "Which is why we don't stop with the refreshed memory. We use it as we would any new lead. To help us find the irrefutable evidence that will put the perpetrator away."

He was making this sound simple, logical. Making it sound like the right thing. Making it sound as if she would be smart to let him do his job. "If I remembered something that helped, would I have to testify at a trial?"

"You might be asked to, yes."

"Would she *have* to?" Kate asked.

"Compelling her to do so wouldn't be my call." Kell turned his attention from her mother to Jamie. "Going into this you should think worst-case scenario to make sure all bases are covered."

Yeah. This was the part she'd been afraid of, what she'd been waiting to hear. She reached for the antacids, stared at the strips of torn wrapper and said, "Worst case being the killer comes after me before he goes to trial."

"That is my bailiwick. And that won't happen."

How could he know? How could he be sure? Things

could go so wrong… "And if I go insane reliving that night, does the court pay my asylum costs? Because as much as I want this bastard behind bars, I'm not sure I won't need bars of my own if those memories come back."

Kate slapped her hand against the table, and dust bloomed in tiny clouds. "Then you're not going to do it. I won't have you spending the rest of your life suffering."

If only it was that simple. Say no, and save herself the horrors those who had lost their loved ones would never put to rest. Or say yes, and hope that closing the case would allow her to do the same.

She looked up at Kell. "If I were to agree, who would do it? Hypnotize me?"

"The Department of Public Safety has officers licensed by the state and trained to use hypnosis in the investigation of crimes. Not a lot. Last I heard, out of sixty thousand officers, only three hundred were certified."

"Would I go to a police station somewhere?"

"You could, or the team would bring the equipment to you."

"Team?" Kate asked.

"The hypnotist, a technician to man the recording equipment and an officer to witness the questioning."

Jamie frowned. "An officer? Not you?"

"I'll be observing, yes, but not in the same room."

Her heart was racing. She didn't know why. She didn't know him well enough to want him there; wouldn't any officer do? "Why wouldn't you be in the same room?"

"I'm working the case—I'm invested in a way the officer witnessing wouldn't be. A neutral witness is best so there's no reaction to what you might reveal."

"And you might react."

He nodded, and she watched his pulse jump at his temple.

Her own jumped in response, then jumped again for reasons that had nothing to do with the case, and everything to do with the look in his eyes. "So it's videotaped, and I can do it anywhere I'm comfortable, and you'll be nearby even if you're not in the room."

"I'll be there, too," Kate said.

"You can observe," Kell was quick to say. "But no family members or anyone connected to the case can be in the room during the session. The rules are set up to make sure the memories recalled are clean, not influenced by observers or by suggestion, that sort of thing. Otherwise, anything recalled is considered tainted, and anything turned up during a follow-up investigation questionable."

"But as long as the rules aren't broken…" Was she that strong? That brave? Would she be able to live with the memories if they came flooding back? Would she be able to live with herself if she didn't give Kell's suggestion a try? She wanted so badly to help; she always had.

All these years, she'd felt so impotent, unable to remember details with enough significance to break the case. Because of her own frustration, it wasn't hard for her to understand that felt by the victims' families. Their accusations had stung, yes, but she'd never taken them to heart. And now she had a chance to give them the one thing they most needed.

How could she not at least try?

Kell had been holding her gaze all this time, and he

finally spoke. "As long as we follow the rules, this is our best shot to shut down this nightmare for good."

We. He'd said we.

Jamie knew her mother was as torn as she was, and that Kate's vote would most likely be no. She didn't want her daughter to have to suffer the horror the refreshed memories could bring. As a mother, that was her right. Kate didn't care that her baby was an adult.

But Jamie *was* an adult. She was the one who had to make this decision, weighing her mother's worries and Kell's assurances against her own counsel.

Really, though, there was only one course of action her conscience would allow her to take—and it would be as much for the other victims as for herself.

"I'll do it."

4

WHILE JAMIE AND HER mother talked privately in the air-conditioned cab of Kate's idling Suburban, Kell walked to the far end of the covered porch where the air stirred by the overhead fan had more room to move.

It was hot, but it was August, and it was Texas, the Chihuahuan Desert swath of West Texas to be precise.

He'd lived in Texas all his life. He'd grown up in Austin where his parents and younger brother still lived. His youngest brother had moved to Houston to work after graduation, exchanging the landlocked central Texas heat for the Gulf Coast humidity. Complaining about the state's weather was as much a part of being a Texan as waving the Lone Star flag.

But the heat sweating its way through Kell now was of a different sort. A heat wrapped up in pink scrub bottoms and long nimble fingers and an intelligence that wouldn't quit. Jamie Danby was an amazing woman, and his gut knotted up thinking of what she'd been through.

Even more gut-wrenching were the questions he kept asking himself. What if the hypnosis backfired and Jamie got burned? What if he got his man, brought him to justice, yet Jamie spent the rest of her life scarred worse than she was now?

He adjusted his sunglasses, staring at the haze fogging his view of the Davis Mountains dipping and rolling in the distance. He owned property on the other side of those hills, in the Guadalupe range, to be exact, a hefty number of acres that were home to coyotes and white-tailed deer and javelinas.

He had a cabin there, a simple log structure where he spent long weekends when he needed to escape the horrors he dredged up and the pain his dredging caused the victims of the original crimes. The sort of hell Jamie would be going through once her mind released its hold on her memories.

She was a cute one, Jamie Danby. Tall and willowy, the scrubs she wore hiding the curves she did have, except for her very fine ass. Her hair was long enough for her to pull up into a ponytail, and though he supposed she'd call it brown, it held a whole lot of dark red. The color probably accounted for the smattering of freckles on her nose and cheeks.

What he liked about her was a combination of things—all of them speaking to the depth of who she was. The way she considered Kate's feelings about the hypnosis; it couldn't be easy to peel back the protective layers her mother had wrapped her in, not knowing what waited on the outside of the cocoon. The way she had chosen to do what was right, though she'd had to fight herself to get there.

He had a feeling she was strong enough to get through whatever happened, but he would damn sure stick around to make sure that she did. That sort of follow-up might not be in his job-description manual, but Kell didn't need a book of rules and regs to tell him how to be human.

Neither did he need a shrink to tell him that his history with the officer who'd fought to keep the case from going cold made his involvement as much personal as professional. He was going to have to toe a fine line, and not cross over into the kind of emotional territory that led to costly mistakes. But that was between Kell and his conscience.

Behind him, one of the SUV's doors slammed closed. He didn't turn, but continued to stare at the rocky mountainside, the trees and scrub growing on the face, their roots finding and clinging to meager patches of soil that neither time nor Mother Nature had eroded away.

Soon enough he heard—and felt—footsteps on the deck as Jamie returned, heard the crunch of ground gravel and the squeal of burning rubber as Kate Danby left her daughter alone with him. Still, he didn't turn. He waited for Jamie to make the first move.

Her agreeing to the hypnosis was huge. He wasn't about to rush or press or insist they had no time to waste. Giving her the time she needed was the best way for Kell to accomplish his goal, and accomplishing his goal was paramount.

Her steps brought her closer. He sensed her at his side, her body heat, her tension, the sound of her sigh. When he caught her scent, his body tightened, and his conscience told him not to be a fool. "It's a rough one. I know."

He didn't, of course. At least not what she was going

through now. Or even what was to come. But he'd made his own share of tough calls, decisions he would rather have not come to. So in that regard…yeah. He knew.

"About that," she said, stepping on the tail end of his thoughts. "What *do* you know?"

He shifted enough that his elbow grazed hers. "What do you mean?"

She stayed there, brushing his shirtsleeve, and followed the direction of his gaze. "Some of the things you said. I get the feeling this case is more than just another left unsolved."

What had he said? What had he let slip? It had to have been something in his tone of voice. He knew he hadn't given anything away with words. She was his reason for being here, and he didn't want her to think otherwise should she discover his connection to the original officer on the case.

"Unsolved cases take a toll. Not that fresh ones don't. They do. I know that." He ran a hand over the back of his neck, wiping at both the stress and the sweat that it— more than the day's temperature—had caused. "But cold cases require the people involved, the victims, the bystanders, the witnesses…they all have to open closed doors, turn keys in locks they thought were keeping them safe."

He kept it at that. Hoped she'd leave it at that. She didn't need to know his professional interest came with a personal bent. The man who'd convinced Kell of his calling, the man who'd been a lifelong friend of his father, deserved better than to have this case go unsolved. But that was Kell's cross to bear. And it was his responsibility to make sure it didn't get in the way of his doing his job.

She didn't respond except to return to their table where she'd left her purse. Kell watched her sling the strap over her shoulder, her expression thoughtful, her eyes beneath frowning brows full of so many things she obviously wanted to know.

He walked toward her, detouring to the opposite side of the table from where she stood. It would be easier to talk to her from here. "Ask me."

Her gaze came up. Her chin, too. She tilted her head to one side, toyed with the end of her ponytail where it fell over her shoulder. He got a kick out of her scrubs top, with its teddy bears wearing firefighter gear, wielding hoses, mounted on ladder trucks.

Finally, she spoke. "I'm not sure you being so perceptive is a good thing or bad." She added a smile; shy, he thought. "I mean, it's good since you're an investigator…"

"But it's bad because it's your case I'm investigating? And I might pick up on things you prefer keeping close to the vest?"

She nodded, released her hold on her shoulder strap and lowered slowly to sit again on the picnic table's bench. "Something like that. Though Roni and Honoria know where I came from and what happened, my mother has made sure that I'm anything but an open book."

And here he was turning her pages. He sat, too.

"It's strange having so few friends to confide in. Living a solitary sort of life." She looked off into the distance, smiling, but for her own benefit, not his. "I was just thinking this morning that I'm a hop and a skip away from turning into a crazy cat lady. Or I would be if I had the cats."

"I hope you're not going to. Hop and skip in that direction." He wanted to give her a reason not to. A reason, instead, to reach for the full life she'd been denied. He couldn't imagine what things had been like for her, existing, not living, within a bubble he doubted was insulated against fear.

She looked back, and shook her head, laughing. "I've been tempted, but so far I've resisted the lure of feline ownership. And of covering a multitude of sins with lace doilies."

She had a sense of humor. Dry, self-deprecating. Even a little bit black. He liked that. Laughter cured a lot of ills. "If this works out, you might just be spared a future of cats, doilies and tea spiked with Jack."

This time when she laughed, it was at his expense completely. "Known a lot of crazy cat ladies, have you?"

She was going to get close. He knew that as surely as he knew he was going to let her. Let her, hell. The way she was hitting his buttons, he'd probably roll out the red carpet before they were done.

"I'm happy to say my experience has been limited to movies and TV."

"Then maybe I'll be your first."

Hoo-boy. The thought of her being his anything… He shook it off. All of it. The temptation, the attraction, the heat that had him wanting to do more than sweat.

He cleared his throat, pulled off his hat and set it on the table, brim up, crown down. "What I'm hoping is that you'll be my first forensic-hypnosis success."

There. He'd successfully switched them back on course. And just as successfully doused her good mood.

"You haven't done this before?" Her voice cracked at the end of her question.

"I'm not the hypnotist, remember? But, no. I've never had cause to use hypnosis on a cold case before."

She looked down, tugged her purse into her lap and held it close, toying with the rings that anchored both ends of the strap. "What if it doesn't work? If I don't remember anything that helps? Or anything at all?"

It was a very good possibility that would be the outcome. He knew that going in. She deserved to know it, too. But the way she'd withdrawn, pulled in on herself as if seeking shelter… She was asking for more than a simple answer.

He'd do his best to give her what would help. "As far as the case goes, I'll rework what's been worked before. New questions, a new investigator, it can make a difference in what memories are jarred. We've got the credit-card receipts from that night. We've got the same from the gas station next door. Those from the motels on either side, too. Someone who was there, working, gassing up, staying the night, stopping for a meal…I hit them again. My angle. My methods."

She was listening. She wasn't looking at him, but she was still, attentive. He took a deep breath and went on. "But as far as what will happen with you…"

Her head came up then, her chin trembling. Tears welled in her eyes and threatened to spill. She reached toward him with one hand, her fingers, her face imploring.

"If I can't remember anything that helps, it'll be hard, but I can live with it. What I can't live with is having to leave here. I'm making it. It's not the life I would have chosen, small town, small job, but I'm happy enough. If that little bit gets taken away…"

She closed her fingers, made a fist, held her lips pressed tight. "This is all I have, Kell. My life in Weldon. I'm safe here. I can't mess that up. I can't start over. There is no starting over."

He wasn't sure why she thought not remembering would mean starting over. What did she think would change? "If you don't remember, things will go on as they have been—"

"No. They won't." She pulled away, sat straighter, taller. She didn't need to dry her tears. They were already gone. "Going on as they have been would require that I not risk the sort of exposure my involvement in your investigation will bring."

"It won't be public—" he started to say, but she cut him off again.

"You can't keep my involvement from going public. You'll try. I know you'll try. But it'll leak out. Someone who knows about it will say something offhandedly, nothing they think twice about. But some listener will pick up on the news, and that spark will become a wildfire that's out of control before you have a chance to blink. You know how these things are, Kell. How they happen."

He did, but he wasn't sure what to say. She seemed certain that whatever the result of the hypnosis, things would change. And since there was no guarantee that her refreshed memories would bring an end to the manhunt—or even give him a place to start—he couldn't argue the validity of her concern.

All he could do was protect her to the best of his ability, and make sure she knew that he would be there anytime she needed him, for as long as she needed him, even after the case was closed.

He circled the table to sit beside her, their thighs close though he faced away from the store while Jamie faced forward. Rather than meet her gaze, he let his nearness assure her while he leaned his forearms on his knees and stared at what he could see of Weldon from here.

The town wasn't small enough that he could stand at the southern city-limits sign and see all the way to the north, but that was only because the main drag took a left and a right before splitting at a fork. One way led to Alpine, the other to Marfa, with not much of Weldon beyond.

Sonora, Texas, the place where Jamie, as Stephanie, had done her growing up was only about three times the size of Weldon, but it wasn't off the beaten path and tucked away in the craggy mountains as was her home for the last ten years.

He understood the lonesome appeal of the place; his cabin was similarly isolated. But he didn't know if he and solitude got along well enough to spend their lives together. He wondered how Jamie did it. He was just about to ask her, when she scooted away.

"I need to get back to work before Honoria and Roni send out a search party." She swung one leg then the other over the bench and stood.

Kell stood, too, hands at his hips. "Do you want me to make the arrangements?"

The look she gave him was full of so much sadness his gut started second-guessing his years of experience.

"How long will it take?" she asked, hitching her shoulder strap higher.

"To set things up? I can do it this afternoon."

"And how soon would it happen?"

"As soon as you want." He couldn't tell if she wanted to get it over with or put it off.

"Tomorrow? Is that too soon?"

Not if it was up to him. "Do you want me to have the team come here?"

"No," she hurried to say, shaking her head vehemently. "I don't want anyone here to know I'm doing this. Or for anything about that night to touch my life here. At least no more than it already has."

He gave a single nod, one of agreement but also of sympathy. Her part was to be brave. His part was to make her bravery easier. "I can set up the session at the Ranger station in Midland."

"That's fine."

He could tell she wanted to get away from this conversation. "I'll get a room for the night and make the arrangements, then give you a call this evening. We can drive up together tomorrow, and I'll bring you back when we're done."

Finally, a smile found its way to her face. "There's not much in the way of overnight accommodations in Weldon. You can try to get a room at the Cordoba Inn, though it's usually booked solid through Labor Day by summer vacationers, as is Indian Lodge. There's the hotel at the state park in Balmorhea, but same thing, especially with the spring-fed pool there, and it's about thirty-five miles away anyway. Of course, there's always my extra bedroom if nothing pans out."

He'd take it. "If I don't have to drive half the day looking for a room, I'll have more time to make sure we can do this tomorrow."

She considered him for a long moment, as if wondering for the same fiery reasons he was how truly wise her offer had been. But rather than take it back, she left it there, an opening, an offer, a heady invitation that ripened in the air simmering between them. "I can walk you over, or we can go back to the clinic for your SUV."

"Why don't we do that," he said, barely able to breathe. "I've got some files I'll need anyway, and my laptop and fax machine."

"Have electronics, will travel?"

"Not to worry," he told her, smiling. "I still carry a gun."

5

BY THE TIME JAMIE made it back to the office, the short clinic day was in full swing, and the hustle and bustle of colds and coughs and ear infections so crazy that she barely had time to think. Neither did she have time—nor opportunity—to tell the story of Kell's visit to Roni and Honoria.

She knew both of her coworkers were curious, but the women also respected Jamie's privacy; they let her know with smiles and quick hugs that anytime she might need them, and for whatever reason, they were there.

Once the noon hour arrived and the clinic's doors were locked for the day, leaving the women the rest of the afternoon free for phone calls and paperwork while Dr. Griñon drove to Alpine to golf, Jamie quickly explained that she'd be taking Thursday and Friday as personal days. Both women were more than willing to pick up the slack while she was gone.

She didn't spell out what it was she would be doing, only that she had to go to Midland to do it. Assuring them she was not in any trouble and there was nothing for either of them to worry about, Jamie worked quietly until five, going through the most pressing items on her desk before heading home.

Where Kell was waiting.

She had tried—and failed—to forget he was at her cottage, sitting at her kitchen table with his laptop, pacing the short hallway while making his calls, perched on the edge of the sofa watching cable news while adding details of their trip to his BlackBerry.

All of that was her imagination, of course, because she had no idea how he'd been spending his time. The only thing she knew for sure was that he'd be staying the night. Just the thought had her slowing her steps as she crossed Brick Avenue and continued her walk to Lamplighter Lane.

As Jamie Danby, she'd had very few men in her life. For a year she'd dated Stuart Pearson who managed the Village Greenhouse Co-op south of town. Stuart had been nice, a great guy, patient and kind, and because he'd been all of those things, Jamie hadn't thought it fair to load him down with her baggage. They'd parted amicably and remained friends; she took the fact that the breakup hadn't caused more than an uncomfortable twinge as a sign she'd done the right thing for both of them.

Things had been much different when she'd still been Stephanie Monroe. During those days, girlfriends, boyfriends and her social life had been her number-one priority. She'd never spent a Friday or Saturday night alone, and spent more weeknights partying than in study or sleep.

It was hard to believe she'd been that girl, to think back on the number of friends she'd had then when she had so few now. And as far as not having men in her life, or even one good man to make her forget those who'd come and gone, well, at least as Jamie she was safe.

Or she had been until Kell Harding had walked into the clinic. Now she didn't know what she was. There wasn't a doubt in her mind that he would do his best to make sure she came to no harm. The doubts crept in when she began to wonder if his best was good enough.

Would anyone's best be good enough? Or was her best bet for keeping danger at bay to continue as she had been, relying on herself and her mother and their combined instincts for survival?

It was the thought of Kate Danby that had Jamie's steps slowing. As much as she owed it to herself—and to the families of those who had died the night she had lived—to help close the Sonora Nites Diner murder case for good, she owed it to her mother most of all.

Kate had given up everything to keep Jamie safe, including the Sonora veterinary practice where she'd gone to work after graduating from Texas A&M, and where she'd eventually become a partner.

For ten years, Kate's life had been Jamie's life, and it was time Jamie released her mother from the obligation to protect her Kate had assumed. Of course, Kate had done so out of maternal love; Jamie got that. But now it was time for the mother to let the daughter give back.

That left only Kell. The part where he was going to work her case wasn't an issue; she was committed to following his lead, his suggestions, his orders. He was a professional, unsolved crimes his business.

No, she found herself dreading the next couple of days in his company because having accepted her fate as a singleton, it wasn't easy to come face-to-face with what she was missing in such a very big way. In such a fit and gorgeous and amazingly kind way.

When she turned the corner onto Lamplighter Lane and saw his big four-wheel-drive vehicle hulking in front of her cottage, she stopped walking and stood there, imagining for a moment what it would be like to come home to that sight every day. Come home to him every day.

Was it something she would ever grow used to? Or take for granted? Having a man like Kell Harding in her life? Being resigned to living alone, she couldn't imagine doing either one, but he wasn't in her life, not in that way, and her daydreaming wasn't productive. She shook it off, continuing down the sidewalk to her back door.

That was when the fantasy and the reality collided. She stopped on the top of the three concrete steps that led from her driveway into her kitchen; the screen door bounced against her rump because she had yet to move. The room smelled like heaven. She rarely cooked. She was one person, easily pleased with a sandwich, and she hated the heat of the stove. But the smell was only half the picture.

The real picture was Kell.

He'd taken over her kitchen. He was tall; his boots made him taller. She'd seen his jeans and white dress shirt before, but this was different. He was in her house, cooking, his long sleeves cuffed up his forearms. He had nice forearms, dusted with dark hair, muscled, a road map of veins in relief beneath his skin.

His hands were large, dwarfing the slotted spoon he held as he lifted home-cut fries from a skillet to drain. He salted them, peppered them, added garlic and what looked like paprika, but could just as easily have been cayenne.

He opened the oven door then, and slid two steaks beneath the broiler before pulling a big bowl of tossed salad from the fridge. That was when he turned, when he killed her with his smile, and with his eyes that twinkled like the stars over the mountains at night.

"Looks like I timed things pretty well."

He had. Perfectly. She came the rest of the way into the kitchen and shut the door on the heat of the day. The heat in the kitchen she could handle. As long as she kept it in the kitchen, and didn't start wondering if Kell was as clever in the bedroom. She was a spinster, remember? And he wasn't here to have sex.

Before she could do more than set her bag on the antique washbasin where she kept her keys and her cell charger, and where she dropped the day's mail, Kell had returned to her cupboards for salad bowls, dinner plates, and grabbed knives and forks from the right drawer without second-guessing.

Just as if he lived here. Just as if he'd been the one to decide where things would go.

She arched a brow, tried not to show all of the appreciation she was feeling. She couldn't let herself get comfortable having him here when it was only for one night. "I see you've made yourself at home."

"Only in the kitchen. I swear," he said, giving her a wink before turning back to the broiler and the steaks. "Well, I did use the facilities, but I washed my hands and aimed true."

Oh God. He was cute, and funny, made jokes at his

own expense, and confident enough to take over her kitchen without asking. She really needed to stop noticing, to remember he was a Ranger sergeant and here for only one thing. And that one thing wasn't dinner, nor was it her.

She headed for the fridge and the pitcher of tea there, was reaching for two plastic tumblers in the cupboard when she and Kell touched. He turned from the stove with the basket of home fries. She took a step in the same direction at the same time, and he reached to stop her from tripping over his feet.

It was nothing but his hand on her arm, his thumb brushing her breast accidentally, yet she felt the shock of electricity deep in her core, saw the same jolt spark in his eyes. She wanted to shake it off, to smile and put the tea on the table, to talk about the weather or the case. He still held her, however, his fingers flexing, as if he didn't know how to let her go, and when he finally did, she sensed regret.

"Sorry about that." He set the fries on the table, and made sure to step around her when he went back to turn the steaks. "I'm used to navigating a one-man kitchen."

She gathered herself close. "Hey, at least you're navigating. I don't do much more than make a beeline through the room to the door."

"You don't cook?" he asked, closing the broiler.

"How much of what we're about to eat, and thank you for that—" she stopped to add along with a nod "—did you have to go out and buy?"

He laughed. "All of it. Well, not the ketchup. Or the salad dressing."

"Exactly. You need condiments, I'm your girl. I can even build a mean sandwich," she hurried on, so the girl thing didn't hang in the air. "But I get my breakfast at Cantus', and usually skip lunch unless Roni or Honoria pack enough for two."

"Let me guess." He leaned a hand on the countertop, parking his other at his hip "They take turns, and it's been years since you've skipped lunch."

"I walk to work," she said before she realized he wasn't commenting on her weight. God, she was not cut out for this…this…banter. Or even small talk. Not with a man who shopped and cooked and set the table, and was going to fix her upside-down life. "I guess they think I don't pack anything so I won't have to carry it with me."

"And you let them think that." He took her in as if there was much about her to be learned in what she'd just said.

She was pretty sure there wasn't much to be learned about her at all, and so she shrugged and poured two tumblers of tea. "I don't want to hurt their feelings. And they both pack a mean lunch."

"Well, I hope my cooking measures up." Kell turned off the broiler to pull out the steaks.

"The way everything smells, that's not a worry." She sat in her regular chair as Kell forked a rib eye onto her plate.

He slid the second onto his own and sat across the table, dropping his napkin into his lap before picking up his fork and knife. "I figured with the lunch meat in the fridge, you weren't a vegan or anything."

Right. Because the lunch meat couldn't be for anyone else. She sighed—though his jumping to the right conclusion about her living alone shouldn't pinch like a nerve. Being unmarried didn't mean she was unmarriageable, but that was her projecting her own issues with being single at thirty, which was her problem, not his.

She loaded her plate down with fries. "One hundred percent carnivore, and this looks so good." She squirted a big pool of ketchup between the potatoes and the meat. "It's almost like you're fattening me up for the kill or something."

Kell remained silent, cutting into his steak and chewing a bite as he sliced off another, frowning all the while as if processing his thoughts as thoroughly as his food. Jamie ate two fries and watched him think, wondering if he would take this much time to respond if she had been anyone other than the sole survivor of a crime.

Finally, Kell laid his utensils along the edge of his plate and sat back, his gaze locking on Jamie's. "Is that how you really feel? That this is all about the hypnosis?"

It was safer to think that way, not to imagine he'd done it for other reasons. Of course, the simplest one was that he'd been hungry…

"That's why you're here, right? And it's not that the meal isn't appreciated." It was so appreciated, he couldn't even know. "I'm just saying, if not for the hypnosis, if you'd just come here to ask me questions to further the investigation, then no. I don't think I'd be sitting down to this feast."

He smiled then, the sort of smile that deepened the laugh lines around his eyes, that had dimples appearing beneath the day's growth of beard on his face. It was a sexy, scruffy look, not the look of a lawman working a case, but that of a man enjoying good food and the company he was keeping. It made Jamie's stomach do all sorts of things, none of them conducive to getting through this meal…or the night ahead.

"If I were here to ask you questions and was making use of your guest room?" He sat forward again, arching a wicked brow. "You can bet I'd be doing then what I'm doing now. For one thing, a man's gotta eat. For another, I'd never be able to face my mother again for fear she'd find out I hadn't properly thanked my hostess."

Mothers. A topic much safer than Jamie giving Kell a bed. "Sounds like your mother raised you right."

Nodding, Kell went back to eating, looking away from Jamie and down at his food. "Mother and father both. They raised three of us boys, and lived to tell the tale."

"Are you the oldest?" she asked, breathing better without his smile stirring her into knots.

"I am," he said, laughing before he asked. "Do I have big brother written all over me or something?"

Brotherly was not at all how she saw him, but she was pretty sure that wasn't what he meant. "You have 'in charge' written all over you. I can't imagine you being the little brother who got bossed around, or the middle child who acted out to find his place."

"Rather deep observations on siblings, coming from an only child."

"What can I say. I paid attention to how my friends fit in with their families while growing up," she said, before finally taking a bite of her mouth-melting steak and barely suppressing a groan.

"And that's why you're working in pediatrics?"

She shook her head. "I'm working in pediatrics because it was the only job I could find after we moved to Weldon."

"What was your major at Tech?"

"How did you know—" She stopped herself, feeling stupid. Of course he would know the details of her life. The case files probably held details not even her mother knew. "I hadn't decided. I was in their general business program, but only because I wasn't sure what I wanted to be when I grew up."

"And?" he prompted.

"Things took an unexpected turn before I ever got my act together," she reminded him, getting back to her food before she confessed things he wouldn't want to hear. He made her want to talk; she didn't know why. But she was pretty sure he wouldn't want to listen to her ramble on about lost dreams.

"What about now?" he asked. "From ten years away. If you could go back to school, what would you study?"

She'd thought many times what she'd give to go back to those days. Not once had she thought about her forgotten degree. "What would Jamie Danby study? Or what would Stephanie Monroe have ended up doing with her life?"

He paused with his fork halfway to his mouth. "Do you not think of yourself as Stephanie?"

"I don't really differentiate between—"

He stopped her from saying more with a knowing shake of his head. "You just did. When I asked about a field of study. You made the distinction between who you are now, and who you were then."

This was something she didn't think she could explain. She'd been Jamie for ten years, Stephanie for nineteen. Sometimes she felt more like one than the other. But always, always, she was both. "Are you the same person you were ten years ago?"

He chuckled. "I'm older, grayer, more stubborn, but mostly I'd have to say yes."

"You've always wanted to be in law enforcement?"

"Since the first time I wore a white hat and straddled a stick horse."

She laughed at that, quickly halted the sound because it rang so strange, then laughed again, unable to help it. She laughed with her mother, she laughed with Roni and Honoria, but this wasn't either of those giggles or girly titters.

This came from the center of her chest. It was deep and heartfelt, and brought on by the picture of Kell as a child riding a broomstick stuck into a stuffed plush head. It felt good. It felt honest.

And she realized that Kell was right. These were Stephanie moments, not Jamie moments. Jamie had been scared, and lonely, for so long. She missed Stephanie's laughter and heart. "I'm sorry. I'm really not laughing at you."

"I'd say that's exactly what you're doing. Or at least doing so at my two-year-old self dressed in nothing but hat, boots and a diaper."

She laughed harder this time, her chest aching, her eyes wet. She didn't know why she found the visual so funny. "Do you have a picture?"

"Even better. I have the video on a DVD. I'll show it to you tomorrow when we're in Midland."

A yanked rug or a thrown bucket of water couldn't have sobered her any faster than the mention of tomorrow's trip. She hadn't wanted to bring the hypnosis to Weldon. This was her home, her sanctuary. She had to keep as much of her past out of her present as she could.

The fact that she was going to have to go back there at all was unsettling, but at least she'd have this place, her place to come back to. Until she didn't anymore.

"Sure. That would be fun." She started to expand her less-than-enthusiastic response, to move on, but Kell reached across the table and took hold of the hand holding her fork.

She looked at his fingers where they spanned from her knuckles to her wrist, felt his thumb where it pressed into the heel of her palm. He was so big, so strong. He could overpower her if he wanted, but all he did was wait for her to meet his probing gaze.

So green, his eyes. Like spring in the mountains. Like leaves unfurling. Like life returning from winter's dead. She felt her throat closing around the words waiting there. This man. He scared her with the way he saw what she was thinking, with the way he made her remember what she'd lost of herself and wanted back.

"It's going to be okay, Jamie. You have every right in the world to dread the unknown, to be frightened of what's coming." He stroked his thumb along her skin as he spoke, tightening his grip on her hand that was shaking. "What you're doing takes enormous bravery."

She blew a sharp snort, pulled her hand free and stabbed her fork into three stacked fries. She couldn't deal with his kindness breaking her down. She needed her armor, Jamie's armor, and she set about pulling it tight. "What about me makes you think I'm brave?"

Kell shrugged, and got back to eating as if nothing had passed between them. "You get up and go to work every day. You do so while looking over your shoulder. And you've done it now for ten years. What about that wouldn't make me think you're brave?"

"The first few years…" She shook her head, toyed with her salad, scooting the multicolored lettuce shreds around on her plate. "I didn't get up every day. I didn't work or go to school. I didn't eat. I honestly don't know how I came out of that darkness with anything left of my mind."

Except she did know. Her mother—her voice, her hands, her heartbeat, her love—had been the only one able to penetrate the inky blackness that had swallowed Jamie whole, that had wrapped tentacles around her, into her, and pulled her away from the light.

"I'm sure Kate had a lot to do with that," Kell said, reaching for his iced tea and staring at Jamie while he drank.

God. Again, he was there with the right words. Kind and perceptive and stealing her breath every time their gazes collided. Jamie nodded. "She had everything to do with it. She's been my rock all these years."

As if entertaining fond thoughts, his expression grew tender. "From what I saw of her earlier, she reminds me a lot of my mother."

A topic of conversation that was safe. She breathed a sigh of relief. "Tell me about her."

Having cleaned all but a strip of gristle and a bite or

two of salad from his plate, Kell sat back. "My folks live in Austin. They retired early. My dad sold his dot-com start-up back when doing so still netted a mint. He golfs. My mom paints. It's a nice life."

"Very cool. Sounds like it would be, retiring when still young enough to enjoy it."

"What about your mother? Would she enjoy an early retirement? Or does she love being a vet too much to hang up her, uh, whatever a vet would hang up?"

Smiling, Jamie reached for Kell's plate, scraped his scraps into hers and carried both along with their flatware to the sink before she answered. "My mother will probably die surrounded by canine testicles and hair balls, a scalpel or laser in her hand."

Obviously fine with Jamie doing cleanup, Kell rocked his chair back on two legs. "Yeah, my mind's eye probably shouldn't go there on a full stomach."

"Sorry," she said with a laugh, bending down for the squeeze bottle of dish detergent beneath the sink. "I forget not everyone grew up talking surgery over dinner."

"Nope. The Hardings talked baseball, football, basketball, girls and food."

"And which sport was yours? Besides the girls?" she asked, turning in time to catch Kell's gaze on her ass. He looked up then, his eyes smoky hot, and she wondered how she was going to get through the night with him sleeping but one room away.

"Football. And baseball. Brennan played hoops and Terry came this close to winning the Heisman," he said, returning his chair to the floor and holding his palms an inch apart.

She loved watching the Olympics every two years, but that was her only interest in sports. "No thoughts of going pro? The lure of the white hat and stick horse too strong? Dazzling dozens of damsels in distress with your big shiny star worth running into the occasional basket case?"

Kell got to his feet, carried the ketchup and salad dressing from the table to the fridge, but he didn't speak until Jamie had filled the sink with soapy water and turned off the tap.

When she looked over her shoulder, she found herself backtracking over what she'd just said. She couldn't find anything wrong…but the flare of temper in Kell's eyes, and the pinch of displeasure around his mouth told a different story.

6

"WHY DO YOU DO THAT?"

"Do what?" Jamie asked, turning back to the sink, though Kell had seen a slip of guilty "ya got me" in her eyes.

She could run, but she couldn't hide—even in a sink of dirty dishes. "Make fun of yourself like that."

She shrugged, a tense roll of one shoulder beneath her teddy-bear scrubs. "I always make fun of myself. It's no big deal."

"Not taking yourself too seriously is one thing. I've seen you do that more than once today. I've seen you get emotional over the situation you're living in and make light of it." He waited a minute to see if she would respond. She did so by turning on the hot rinse water full blast. "But putting yourself down is not the same thing."

"Ten hours, and you know me so well."

He reached around her to shut off the gushing splash of water. He hadn't been ready for the silence, her stillness, her pain. The way she smelled like soap made of grapefruit and lemon zest. The sadness surrounding her.

He knew he should move, should give her space and time to work through what she was feeling, but he stayed close, noticing the fine hairs that curled into copper pennies at her nape. "I don't know you. But I know crime. I know people. I know…victims."

She bristled, tightened, lifted her chin to look out the window over the sink, but didn't look at him. He moved to her side, leaning an elbow on the countertop to get a look at her face. "I know you don't think of yourself that way, that you think of the people who died, of Kass Duren and Lacy Rogers and Julio Alvarez and Elena Santino as the victims. Of the Duren and Rogers and Alvarez and Santino families as the ones who suffered the most."

"They did suffer the most," she shouted, whipping her gaze toward him, her ponytail flying with the motion of her rage, her eyes angry, hurt.

He shook his head, softened. "They got the most sympathy. They were painted in the press as heart-broken. They lost loved ones. But your suffering has been just as great. You lost friends. You lost your innocence. You were accused of keeping things from the authorities. You had your life ripped away like a bandage off an open wound. I would say you've suffered just as much as anyone else."

She hung her head, leaned forward on hands that were buried to her wrists in sudsy water. "I should have died. I played dead. He thought I was, and left me there. I should have died."

Survivor's guilt. Common. Not unexpected. And such a burden for her to have carried for ten years. Kell hoped he wasn't about to make things worse. "I'll bet your mother's glad you didn't."

"She is," Jamie said, choking back a sob.

"I'll bet you're glad, too."

She nodded, squeezing her eyes shut as tears dripped to salt the dishwater and her skin.

"It's okay to be glad, Jamie." He straightened, took a step closer.

She shook her head, saying nothing. She didn't have to. He knew from interviewing victims as part of his work with the UCIT the things going through her mind. Knew, too, many who had given up.

"I'm sorry that I opened the old wounds. Hurting you wasn't my intent."

"I know that," she said, snuffling softly and hunching a shoulder to wipe her eyes and nose. "It's okay. I'll be fine."

He thought she would be, thought, too, that revisiting the past would enable her to get rid of it for good. That didn't mean it was going to be a painless process. But he wasn't going to push beyond what was needed. He wouldn't. That much he swore.

He hesitated, but in the end couldn't bear to see her crushed, so he wrapped an arm around her shoulders and pulled her into his chest. She didn't want to lean, shaking the soapy water from her hands and sniffing back tears. He handed her a dish towel and didn't let her go.

They stood like that for several moments, looking through the window and past her driveway to her neighbor's property beyond, Jamie finally relaxing, her breathing growing steady and deep. Kell remained where he was, letting her move away even though he could've stayed there a lot longer.

"Wow," she finally said, brushing back her hair with

one wrist and getting back to the dishes. "Sorry about the meltdown. You would think after all this time my armor would be completely without chinks."

It said a lot that it wasn't, and as he set about clearing the rest of the dishes and food from the stovetop and table, he had high hopes that her vulnerability would lead to success tomorrow—no matter how mercenary it sounded.

THE BED IN JAMIE'S GUEST room was a full and required Kell sleep with his head at the top left, his feet at the bottom right. He didn't sleep a lot, but he couldn't blame the size of the mattress. Not completely.

He'd been known to sleep in the driver's seat of his SUV, on the ground without a sleeping bag, in his chair at the office for a quick take five. Tonight, his inability to get to sleep and stay there was due in a large part to anxiety about tomorrow.

It was due even more to the woman asleep in the room next to his, and the things he was feeling about her, because of her, for her, even. Things that had nothing to do with her cold case, and yet had everything to do with who she was because of what had happened in the diner that night.

He'd studied the crime scene photos repeatedly, read through her statement so many times that, lying here now in his boxer briefs, covered to the waist by a sheet and cooled by the ceiling fan, the events of that night played in his mind as if he'd been there to see it unfold.

Jamie had been behind the counter running the day's register tapes, and counting and bagging the money in the till to drop in the bank's night deposit. The lights in the diner had still been burning, the neon sign above the front door spelling out Closed in a nostalgic red font.

Julio Alvarez and Elena Santino had been out front mopping the black-and-white-tiled floor and scrubbing down the white Formica tables and red Naugahyde booths.

Kass Duren and Lacy Rogers had been scouring the kitchen, storing food, gathering the trash to take to the Dumpster. The bags and cans, spattered with Kass's and Lacy's blood, had still been sitting by the back door when the authorities arrived.

Julio and Elena had crumpled one on top of each other, their blood pooling into a shared circle of death. Jamie had been spared from seeing her friends die, having dropped to the floor when the first shots were fired.

The bullet that had grazed her scalp and the one that had gouged her shoulder had bloodied her and the floor around her enough to fool the killer into thinking she was dead. But she hadn't been dead. She'd been quite alive, drifting in and out of consciousness, hearing the screams, the pleading, the voices choking in terror, drowning as her friends died.

His chest and throat tight, Kell tossed off the sheet and sat up, reaching for the jeans he'd left on the floor. He pulled them on, needing fresh air, water, a long walk with only coyotes and javelinas and the moon to watch. What he didn't need was to think about Jamie revisiting the scene he'd just imagined. And doing it because of him.

He headed for the kitchen, barefoot and shirtless, figuring he could grab a glass of water, take it outside, and pace her driveway for now. If that didn't help, well, a sleepless night wouldn't kill him. He had his laptop. He could go over his notes and files again and—

The kitchen should've been dark, but the back door stood wide open, allowing the light of the moon to spill through. His first thought was his gun, his second, Jamie. But a couple of silent steps into the room and he saw her sitting outside on the concrete stairs that rose to the back door, a bottle at her hip, a glass in her hand.

Uh-oh.

He made sure she heard his next steps. He even nudged a chair with his hip, scraping the legs on the floor and knocking it against the table. Jamie startled, but quickly settled, reaching for the bottle and hiding it between her feet. Tried to hide it, anyway.

Kell stood in the doorway behind her. "You planning to drink all of that yourself?"

"Grab a glass," she told him, scooting forward and leaning over enough for him to get through the screen door without pushing her off the top step.

He found a bottle of water and a glass that he filled with ice, and joined her. The night was warm, clear, the stars overhead like tiny twinkling Christmas-tree lights. It was a good night to get drunk. Tomorrow's agenda made it an even better one—except tomorrow's agenda required sobriety, ergo, the water and ice.

"Can't sleep?" A stupid question since here they both were, barefoot and half dressed, Jamie wearing a skinny-strapped tank top with pajama shorts that came nearly to her knees. He thought they were blue, but they might've been a soft green. He thought, too, that she wasn't wearing a bra.

She lifted her glass. "I will soon."

He reached for the liquor bottle between her feet, poured just enough into his glass to balance the ice then added water, offering her the same. She gave a nod, and he diluted her drink to match his, keeping his mouth shut. This wasn't the time to preach. Besides, he couldn't blame her for wanting to take the edge off.

"The nights are my favorite part of living in West Texas," she said after sipping her drink. "It's so quiet. And so clear. Have you seen the stars from the observatory?"

The McDonald Observatory, on top of Mount Locke and Mount Fowlkes, was about seventeen miles away, and provided astronomers some of the darkest night skies in the forty-eight contiguous states. "I have. Amazing the things the human eye can see with nothing in the way. Satellites, the Hubble, the International Space Station."

"And those are all man-made. Think how much farther away the constellations and even the Andromeda Galaxy are." She sipped again, swirling the liquid in her glass. "It sounds stupid, but even if things hadn't gone so wrong, I don't think I'd have ever moved away from this part of the country. I love the nights too much."

"Too bad the days are so miserable," he said, though really, living in Texas meant living with the heat, and he was Lone Star born and bred.

"You grew up here, right? You should be used to it."

He nodded, and swirled the ice in his glass. "I am, but weather always makes for easy conversation."

For a moment, she was silent, then she sighed with a deep resignation. "Easier than asking why I can't sleep?"

Or telling her what was keeping him awake. He nodded, sipped the Jim Beam and let it warm the parts of him left cold by the thoughts that had driven him from bed.

Jamie stretched out her legs, spread her toes, then bent to brush away something he couldn't see. "I don't lose a lot of sleep anymore over…everything. At first, I didn't think I'd ever sleep again. I had a prescription that helped. Or it did once my doctor upped the dosage a couple of times."

"Made for some fuzzy days I bet." He sat forward, his wrists on his knees, looking away from the smooth skin of her legs toward her detached garage and the moon shining in the windows there.

"Time was a big blur for months. I couldn't go back to school. I couldn't work. I did good to eat and bathe myself, though it took a while to care enough to do even that." She brought her glass to her mouth. "I honestly don't think I would've come out of it if my mother hadn't been with me."

She'd been so young, a kid, really. A very young woman at most. Either way, she'd been a girl who'd needed her mother, and had been lucky to have one so devoted. "She sounds pretty amazing."

"You have no idea." Jamie sat straighter, stretching her back, left then right, popping her spine before she leaned back against the frame of the screen door. "She did all of it herself, the taking-care-of-me stuff. Making sure I got through."

He'd known from her file that her father had split about that time, but didn't know the why. The way she said it… "Was it too much for your dad…what happened to you?"

"Something like that. I guess." She lifted her glass, and stared at the contents where the moonlight glinted off the amber liquid. "It's always been weird the way he bailed."

"How so?"

"He'd been a perfect dad my whole life, though somewhat taciturn, I guess. He helped with my science homework and showed me how to fix a flat on my bike. Oh, and how to run the lawn mower."

"The lawn mower?"

"I was the son he never had, taking care of a lot of things around the house while he and the seasonal workers handled the ranch chores."

Kell found himself chuckling. "Terry, my baby brother, got the same treatment. Except in reverse."

"How so?"

"My mother was determined one of her children would cook. Terry was the youngest, left behind when Brennan and I were in school, so he had a lot of one-on-one time with Mom." He stared down at the concrete step between his feet, his bare soles soaking up the stored heat from the day. "It seems to have stuck."

"He's a cook?"

"He owns a restaurant. A pub. In Houston. Not sure he still does much cooking, but he has. And he can."

"Runs in the family then."

"The steaks?" He shook his head. "That's bachelor food. Steaks, burgers, eggs. Nothing but the basics."

She was quiet for the next couple of minutes, not drinking, not moving, just sitting, letting the night wrap them in its cloak, letting the darkness keep them rooted, letting the heat of the drink lull them into a sense of easy comfort until the solitude finally loosened her tongue.

"Have you always been a bachelor?"

"I've never been married, if that's what you're asking."

"Why not?"

He guessed she was waiting for him to tell her he'd never found the right girl. Wasn't that usually the reason? And while it was true, it wasn't the whole story of why he was alone. "I haven't had the time to invest in a relationship. Not that sort of time."

"That sort of time? What do you mean, that sort of time?" She leaned across him to snag the bottle from where he'd set it on his side of the steps. Her unbound breasts, firm, full, brushed his knees. "You make it sound like a job, or a chore. Like work."

What he was working on right now was keeping his hands wrapped around his glass of throat-searing whiskey and melting ice. He wanted so badly to touch her. "You don't think relationships are work?"

"I wouldn't want to go into one thinking that, no." She sat forward again, gesturing with her glass. "I mean, I watched my mother work her ass off to salvage what she had with my father. She wheeled and dealed and begged, even agreed to let him do his man-alone-with-nature thing while she took care of me. He left anyway. Just loaded up his truck and his horse trailer and drove off into the sunset."

Hmm. Was she basing her feelings about relationships on one couple? Her parents? She had to know that marriages rarely survived something so horrific as what had happened to their child. Or…wait. Was Jamie blaming herself for her father's desertion?

Kell looked over at the strands of hair blowing into her face, catching on her lips and lashes. He reached for them, brushed them back over her shoulder, but then he let his hand linger there, let his fingers drift softly over the skin beneath her ear.

It was a big mistake, touching her, and even though he pulled away, he knew he'd done so too late. He'd crossed a line he shouldn't have, and even if he'd wanted to he could never go back. "If your father didn't work just as hard, then their marriage didn't stand a chance. There are two people in a relationship, and if only one is working, it's hard to imagine that it wouldn't fail."

Jamie sat shaking her head, before pushing to her feet and walking to the center of the driveway, as if she'd reached her limit on sitting still. She wobbled a bit, swayed a bit more, found her footing and stood in profile, her hair lifting on the warm night wind.

The moon bathed her; Kell could see the globes of her breasts, her nipples, the long line of her back to the gorgeous swell of her rump, the hint of her sex beneath the cotton of her pjs that was very very thin. Just like she wasn't wearing a bra, she wasn't wearing panties.

"The problem with my parents' relationship is that it grew to be about a third person, not just the two my father signed on for. The third, me," she said again, this time her voice cracking like glass, "was what ended up tearing them apart."

Kell didn't know the details, he had no right to assume or intrude. But Jamie's state of mind was a crucial component in what he was hoping would be tomorrow's success—though he knew what was going on here, tonight, between them had nothing to do with the case.

"It wasn't your fault, Jamie—"

"Of course it was," she shouted back, the sound like an explosive blast in the stillness.

If she'd had neighbors living close, he would've expected lights in windows to come on, curtains to sweep aside, concerned eyes to peer out and see if she needed help. But her closest neighbor on Lamplighter Lane was half a block away, and the house remained quiet and still.

Inside, Kell was anything but, his stomach and heart battling a surge of emotion, and he had to force his frustration into calm. "If your father left because of what happened to you, it was his problem, not yours. You were in the wrong place at the wrong time. That's all."

"A wrong place he didn't want me to be," she said, and finished off her drink, heaving her glass toward the garage, where it shattered, the slivers and shards scattering on the pavement.

Kell didn't move. He waited—though he would stop her if she even thought about cleaning up the glass. She was barefoot, a little bit drunk, and it was dark in the shadow of the garage.

She stayed where she was, however, dropping down and wrapping her arms around her knees, rocking back and forth, her back and shoulders arched like a turtle's protective shell.

So her father hadn't wanted her to work at the Sonora Nites Diner? Because of the late hours? Because of the easy access to the interstate? Because he'd wanted her to focus on her studies? Kell hadn't met her father, had only read about Steven Monroe's abandonment years after the fact. He had no way of knowing what the issue was between Jamie and her father.

He did know that it was time for sleep. For Jamie, and for him, too, so he capped the bottle, set his glass beside it next to the steps and went to bring her inside.

7

JAMIE KNEW BETTER than to drink. She had no tolerance for alcohol. She was an easy drunk, the cheapest of cheap.

And a barefoot Kell Harding, wearing nothing but his jeans, was going to make her cheaper and easier than she'd been in years. She could feel it in her blood, in her bones, a fire of lust and stupidity and Jim Beam.

She knew he was standing in front of her, but she kept her eyes closed. It had been hard enough not to touch him when he'd been sitting on the stoop beside her. She could smell him then, and now.

He'd showered before bed, and the heat of the night had carried the scent of his clean skin until she wanted to crawl beneath it, and wrap it around her like a cloak, and remember what it had been like to live without looking over her shoulder. She wanted that back, all of it.

"Let's go in. You need sleep. I need sleep. The glass will wait till morning."

Still hunkered down, she shook her head. "If I sleep, I'll dream, and it won't be one I can stomach alone. Not tonight. Not with…all of this happening. And with tomorrow." *Don't cry, don't cry, don't cry,* she told herself. *Please, please, don't cry.*

"I'll be in the next room. And I'll be with you tomorrow." He touched her hair then, brushed his knuckles against her temples. "I'm here now."

But he wasn't here in the way she needed him. He was here as a cop, a watchdog, here to keep her smart and sober and on time, though he was running late on the first two counts. She grabbed his wrist to stop him from moving his fingers along the shell of her ear, using her hold as leverage to gain her feet, rising along his body.

And then she couldn't help it. He was in front of her, looming, his chest big, bare and magnificent and calling her. She placed her hands there, the heels of her palms just beneath his pectoral muscles, her fingertips skating the edges of his nipples.

The wedge of hair in the center of his chest was soft, thinning as it descended his abdomen. She followed it with her thumbs, her eyes wet, her cheeks wet, her belly tight with wanting him, with wanting.

He stopped her when she reached his waistband. She felt him there, just beneath, swelling, full and firm, but he kept her from enclosing him in her hand, and held her arms at her sides. "Not a good idea."

His body said otherwise. "Are you sure? I'm getting some mixed signals here."

"I'm sure," he told her, his grip tightening when she tried to pull away and prove him wrong. "Another time, another place, maybe."

"You're saying no because of tomorrow?" Not because she was an old maid, damaged and broken and lost, with nothing to offer a man? Not because she was ugly and drunk and pathetic? Not because he didn't want her?

"I'm saying no because we both need sleep," he re-iterated, his voice rough, rougher than the hands holding her, than the concrete driveway she was standing on. "And because the reasons right now are all wrong."

What did that mean? That he could only tumble her into forgetfulness if it fit his white-hat sense of right and wrong? How fair was that, when she was the one who wanted no strings attached?

She pulled against his efforts to keep her at a distance, lifting her hands to his chest again, to his shoulders, lacing them around his neck.

She shimmied close, pressed her nipples to his chest and rubbed against the cotton of her camisole until sensation swept her to the edge of oblivion. "What do the reasons matter?"

He groaned. The rumble rose from a spot just beneath his ribs and made it all the way up his throat before stopping. His heart drummed, a thudding, primal, near-violent beat. "We can't. Not now. Not…like this. Here. It's late. You've been drinking."

Exactly. She could do anything she wanted to do. She had Jim Beam on her side. Eyes closed, she leaned her forehead against him and breathed.

His chest hair tickled her nose, her lips. She licked them, caught the edge of his nipple and licked that, too, smelling the alcohol in his pores, the heat of the night, something wholesome and sweet. All of it right, and hers.

"Jamie."

He ground out her name like a curse. Or a caress. She wasn't sure which one. She didn't care. She brought her mouth to the hollow of his throat, drank of his taste and his scent. He lowered his head, nuzzling his chin to her temple.

It was soft, but it was still need, and she turned into it, finding his mouth, biting until he parted his lips and bit back. Oh, he was going to be good, greedy and giving, hungry, hard.

She cupped his head, kneading the nape of his neck as she kissed him, her tongue on his, her chest against his, her sex aching where the ridge of his pressed, his hands on her ass lifting her like a puzzle to fit his pieces.

It was her whimper that ruined everything. He was hard everywhere, his fingers bold and questing, and it had been so very long since she'd wanted anyone to touch her as intimately as Kell was doing now. And so she whimpered, but just barely, with pleasure and need and an appreciation for the bad-boy way he kissed.

Kell's hands on her bottom stilled, then dropped her cheeks like two hot potatoes. He broke the kiss, found her wrists and broke her hold on his neck, cursing to himself as he took a step away. His face was in shadow, but his darkness was more than the lack of light.

He was angry. At her? At himself? And his whole body raged, stiff and tight and pulsing. "I said no, Jamie. Not here, not now, not without a better reason than dreading tomorrow."

If he didn't think dreading tomorrow was reason enough, then he was right that this wasn't the time or place. And he wasn't the man. Good thing Jim Beam wasn't so righteous.

"Good night then, Ranger Sergeant Kellen Harding," she said, walking away with a wobble, but without a single look back, and picking up the whiskey bottle before opening the screen door. "I'll do whatever it takes to deal with tomorrow. And I'll get help from whomever will give it."

No matter how very very much I want it to be you.

KELL HAD ARRANGED FOR Jamie's session with the forensic hypnotist to happen in Midland at eleven. The hypnosis was their sole purpose for making the trip; there was no excuse to put it off until later in the day.

The claustrophobic three-hour drive would've had her worrying herself into a state of exhaustion had she not been struggling to keep her stomach from upending all over the floor of Kell's SUV.

Spending the night with Jim Beam had not been particularly smart, but it had worked as a preemptive strike against freaking out; all she had on her mind this morning was not getting sick. Thankfully, Kell hadn't brought up her drinking, or anything about last night.

"I don't drink like that very often." She closed her eyes, opened them quickly when her nausea insisted on looking at something besides the blood-red interior of her eyelids.

"That's good to know." And that was all he said, his right hand on the steering wheel, his left elbow on the padding where the window met the door. His face was close shaved, his shirt starched and pressed. He wore his white hat and dark sunglasses. Jamie hadn't seen his eyes all day.

He hadn't had as much to drink last night as she had, so she didn't know if he was hiding bloodshot whites or dark purple half-moons beneath. Maybe he just didn't want her to know when he cut his gaze toward her, if he did, how often, how thoroughly he looked her over, what he was visually searching for. Maybe he just didn't want her to see his disillusionment.

"I mean, I'm not an alcoholic or anything. I drink sometimes, when I can't sleep." Or when I do sleep and the nightmare comes back.

"You don't have to justify anything to me, Jamie."

Right. He was going to turn her life upside down, but didn't want an explanation for her reaction to having that happen. Well, she didn't want him looking back and thinking her a slutty little lush.

"I'm not justifying anything, Kell. I'm explaining what went on last night, what you saw. That wasn't… me," she said, though the words rang false because the woman he'd seen was exactly who she was.

She put on a good front for her mother, her neighbors, her coworkers and friends, the world, but the real truth was too sad and broken to let anyone see. Anyone, apparently, but a man in a white hat with a gun.

He looked over at her, his jaw taut, his mouth grim. She couldn't see his eyes or his forehead, but could tell his face wasn't happy. She could tell, too, from his voice that was gritty and sharp. "Don't you think I get that? Yeah, we just met, but I know your case inside and out, and that includes the person you are."

She wanted to believe him, but it sounded a lot like he was making nice to get her to shut up about it. And, really, she wanted to shut herself up about it. She didn't know why it mattered so much that he think good things about her.

Except she did know. It mattered because of that kiss. Last night's blood-alcohol level hadn't kept her from remembering, reliving the feel of his mouth, his hands, his…everything dozens of times since rolling her protesting body out of bed this morning.

She wanted to kiss him again. She wanted to kiss him while sober. She wanted to kiss him in broad daylight or with the room's lights blazing. She wanted to kiss him and remember things the Jim Beam meant she'd forgotten.

None of that would happen, however, until he remembered something other than his disappointment in her. At least she assumed it was disappointment that had him keeping such a stiff distance between them.

"Did all that reading about me make you curious?"

"About?"

Oh, now he was being purposefully thick. "Anything in particular? What author I most like to read, or my favorite restaurant, or where I've traveled, or if I like to go fishing, or maybe know how to kiss?"

The corner of his mouth twitched. His hand on the steering wheel tightened, his knuckles like jagged peaks. "Who's your favorite author?"

Sigh. It was better than talking about the weather, or traveling in complete silence, though she'd much rather know what he thought about kissing her. "I'd have to say Tess Gerritsen. She writes a suspense series about a Boston police detective and medical examiner."

"Hmm."

"What does that mean, 'hmm'?"

He shrugged, continued to face straight ahead.

"I would've thought you'd prefer something less…
gruesome."

Because of what she'd been through? "It's storytell-
ing. It's entertainment. I'm not looking to forget what
happened to me by escaping my reality. Or to work my
way through it by projecting my experience onto a piece
of fiction. It's just…reading."

"If you say so."

He didn't buy it, or else he was being contrary to keep
her at bay. And that really didn't make any sense when
everything else he'd done was about keeping her
close…unless the kiss had made him change his mind.

"What's your favorite restaurant then?"

Fine. She'd play along, but only because she wanted
to see if he'd make it through all five of her options, or
if he'd stop when he reached the last one. "I'm not sure
I have a favorite, but there's one in Junction called
Isaack's where the cheeseburgers are the best I've ever
had in my life."

He chuckled at that, a funny, rough sound, glancing
in his side-view mirror before signaling and changing
lanes. "How do you feel about fishing?"

Moving right along here…though he'd skipped
asking about where she'd traveled. Was he in a hurry to
talk about kissing her? Or just wanting to get it over with
ASAP? "I've never been."

That earned her a glance, one she couldn't read
because he was still hiding behind his dark glasses.

"I'm not sure I've ever met anyone who's never
fished," he told her, then asked, "No opportunity, no
interest, what?"

"Both, I guess. Though I've eaten my fair share of things that live in the sea. And lakes, streams, rivers, swamps."

"Swamps?"

"Crawfish. Frog legs. Alligator. You know. Swamp things."

Kell shook his head, giving a soft snort that she interpreted as disbelief. He didn't seem the type to be disgusted by things that weren't everyday food. "You've never been fishing, but you've eaten frog legs and alligator."

"I didn't have to catch them, just order them," she said, her headache easing along with some of the tension causing the drive to be so uncomfortably difficult. Funny how talking helped simplify things, when keeping them bottled up and hidden away made a more "out of sight, out of mind" sense.

And, no, she was not going to stop and apply that realization to the last ten years of her life. Or wonder why she'd talked more about what she'd seen and suffered to Kell Harding than she had to another soul in years. Crawfish and frog legs and alligator. That was the ticket, the always safe subject of food.

She leaned into the corner of the seat, shifting to see him better. "In case you didn't notice at dinner, I've got a big thing for food. I'll try anything, and I love almost everything. My mouth was definitely made for eating."

"That must be why you taste so good."

And just like that, there was the kiss.

8

THE KISS. They had to get it out of the way or today was going to be a bust, which was why Kell had put it out there. Thinking about Jamie's hypnosis to come had gotten lost in thinking about her mouth. But she was wrong.

Her mouth was not made for eating.

It was made for the way she'd used it last night, and he was surer than he was about never wanting to eat alligator, that she could use it for even more. Those things, all intimately imagined, were giving his body hell.

"I don't think I've ever had anyone tell me that I taste good," she finally replied, and as he glanced over, he saw her face color with the implications of what she'd just said. "Though I'm sure it had something to do with the JB."

Nice recovery, he thought, amused, though they both knew he hadn't been talking about the booze. "I swear, Jamie. If it had been any other time or place…"

He let the sentence trail, not sure why he was giving even more air to the subject instead of allowing it to breathe its last and drift off to die. Unless that wasn't what he wanted, to let it go, to forget.

"Yeah. You said that last night," she reminded him.

"I wasn't sure you heard me."

"I was drunk, but I was right there."

"I know." Where she'd been, the way she'd tasted, how she'd felt in his hands would stick with him a long, long time. "I just wanted to make sure we were clear."

"Oh," she said, then after a pause, went on to ask, "Why aren't you in a relationship? I mean, I'm assuming you're not…"

"I'm not, no, and I guess for the same reason I'm not married. My mother nags about grandchildren, but I'd rather not tackle parenthood on my own." His line of work had convinced him of that, as had his childhood. Sure, some single parents did a better job than two, but he wasn't cut out to try it.

Smiling, Jamie tucked her feet beneath her to sit cross-legged. "Your mother and my mother must be reading from the same script."

He wondered if what she'd been through had changed how she felt about starting a family. Maybe she'd never wanted one at all. Maybe she wanted one now more than ever. He didn't ask because he didn't want to stir things that had settled.

But then she went on. "The married-with-children thing is a long-running joke between me and my mother. She takes the blame for me being single."

Coming up on a slow-moving vehicle, Kell eased the SUV's cruise control to coast before changing lanes. It gave him time to let what Jamie had said sink in. "Why would she think it's her fault?"

"Because of her hovering."

Strange, he mused, passing the car on his right, the sun

that shone through the window glinting red through Jamie's hair. "She seemed concerned, protective even, but I didn't get a sense of her hovering. Or of you letting her."

Jamie laughed, a wonderful sound, fearless and full of life. "Trust me. There's no letting involved. She does it. I put up with it. And we love each other to death. End of story."

"Love makes all the difference," he heard himself saying before he thought better of going soft. "Between crowding and caring, I mean."

"It can still be crazy-making," she said, the smile on her face wry.

Kell understood. He had a few crazy-making memories of his own. "I lucked out being the oldest. My mom still had Terry and Brennan at home to fuss over. Then Brennan left for school and Terry got the full baby-of-the-family treatment."

Jamie chuckled. "And you weren't jealous at all."

"Jealous?" He shook his head. He didn't begrudge either of his brothers anything. "But I did miss the attention." And then he heard himself admitting, "I liked being spoiled. Still do."

Several seconds passed before Jamie responded, and Kell began to wonder what the hell he was doing. Getting the kiss out of the way had been one thing. Turning the conversation back to the personal was another, and not very smart.

He did not like the direction the attraction between them was driving him. He'd told her twice now another time, another place, and was thinking he should tattoo a reminder on the inside of his eyelids, a road sign telling him where not to go before he found himself unable to shift gears.

Finally, she moved, shifting in her seat, her voice low when she said, "The right woman will do that, you know. Spoil you."

It wouldn't do any good to pretend she was talking about someone's mother when she was talking about all the things he'd wanted from her last night, the things he'd denied himself, the things he could've had right there in her driveway.

He couldn't let himself think she was making him an offer, or read anything into the one she'd made him last night. She was a case he was working. That's all they had between them. "Yeah? The right woman and a Faustian bargain?"

She sat back with a huff. "No wonder you're still on your own."

He wanted to laugh, to tease her, to play until they reached their destination, but mostly he was desperate for a way out of this detour, so he grabbed the opening she'd given him instead. "I'm not so good at leaving my work at the office. I've never thought it would be fair to saddle someone with my life, what I have to deal with, what I see. I'm not always the best of company."

He knew she would understand his concern. Because of what she'd lived through, it had to be something she'd considered. He didn't for a minute believe she'd never been in a relationship, though he wouldn't be surprised if her lovers had been only casual.

Anything more would mean letting someone in, and neither one of them lived in a place that was very inviting. Jamie lived with the horror of her past, and would for the rest of her life; even if the killer was caught and put away, she'd carry with her what had happened.

And Kell… He carried his cases in his head; his subconscious was always stewing on the ones he'd back-burnered while he feverishly stirred those that were hot, leaving very few of his brain cells for anything else.

Funny when he thought about it, but in a lot of ways, he and Jamie were two of a kind, their lives forever bound to the heinous offenses of others. It sucked in so many ways.

"So it's easier to be a martyr than to trust a woman to have what it takes to deal. Is that it?"

Biting down on a lot of words best left unsaid, Kell maneuvered toward the Midland exit. He knew he should've kept his mouth shut, because now he was going to have to go on the defensive, and that was not the mood he'd been working so hard to set. "It's not about being a martyr. Or about trusting or not."

"Then what's it about?" she demanded, because she obviously couldn't leave the subject alone.

He decided to turn it back on her, let her spin it from her own point of view. "Don't you find it hard to let men get close?"

She looked away from him and stared out her side window as they passed the Midland city-limits sign. And then she crossed one leg over the other and scooted closer to the door. Since she'd answered with her body, he didn't expect her to give him a verbal response.

"I let you get close. I would've let you get even closer if you hadn't put a stop to things."

He knew that. The reminder was not exactly welcome when he was trying to forget what he'd said no to. "I'm not talking about…sex."

"I know. You're talking about emotional intimacy. Caring and affection and eventually love. And, yes, I have found that hard. Mostly because I'm very careful when talking about my past." She paused, pushing the hair she'd left hanging loose away from her face. Color tinted her cheekbones, as if her admission didn't come easy. "It's been a deal breaker more than once. Men ask, I refuse to answer, they think I'm hiding something. They're right, but I'm not going to risk exposing myself just so some guy feels better about what he's getting into. A guy wants something long-term, he should be willing to accept my timetable for sharing what happened."

A knot of anger balled like a fist in Kell's stomach. He knew men like the ones she was describing, men who demanded everything go their way, men who made it hard for women to cut the rest of the male gender a break, a few of whom deserved to be strung up by what passed for their balls.

He started to tell her she deserved better, that the right man would be there for her past, present and future, but stopped. He didn't want the sentiment to come out sounding as patronizing as he feared it would. Besides, he felt strangely protective, possessive even, and didn't buy it when he told himself it was all about the case.

Before he could round up what he was feeling and force it into some kind of sense, Jamie took a deep breath and went on. "The thing is, making an intense connection with someone who knows those things about me, even one tangled up with a dark night, a bottle of JB and a killer kiss… Let's just say, it's not something I'm going to walk away from. And I'm sorry you felt you had to."

Kell was only human, and he couldn't take it anymore. He swerved the SUV into a parking lot, slammed on the brakes and shoved the transmission to park. His chest heaving, he stared straight ahead, his hands gripping the steering wheel so he didn't reach for her. "A little late to be spelling out the rules, don't you think?"

She gave a sarcastic grunt. "Better late than never. Besides, last night I was too self-involved to think you might need a playbook."

That didn't sit well. His blood began to boil. "I know all the plays, Jamie. I just don't like running them when I'm the only one with his head in the game."

Jamie was leaning toward him, a move that gave him a really good look down the front of her shirt. A gentleman would have looked away.

Kell was no gentleman. He unhooked her seat belt and pulled her to sprawl across his lap, reached for her breasts and brought his mouth down hard on hers. She pushed his hands away and unbuttoned her blouse. He felt her smile as his erection swelled to bump her thigh, and he wasn't sure which of them groaned the loudest.

The fire they'd set last night had burned. This fire exploded, an incendiary rush of heat and flame that sucked them both into its back draft. Jamie's mouth was hungry, her lips and teeth and tongue involved, her free hand warm against his cheek and holding him still.

This was wrong. So very wrong. But there was no way Kell was going to move when nothing in his life had felt this right. Jamie was a case, a victim of a crime, his job. He had no business wanting her at all, much less in ways that had him losing his mind. Yet he didn't care.

How could he when she fit him and wanted him and kept him from being able to draw enough breath? Men dreamed of this. Men paid for this. Hell, men killed for this. And here it was his, and all he'd done was broil her a steak and share her Jim Beam beneath the light of the moon.

Her breast in his palm was sweetly heavy, rounded like a peach, ripe and firm. He cupped and molded, leaving the fabric of her bra as a barrier teasing them both. She wiggled against him, pressed against him, nipped at his lower lip to tell him to move it out of the way. He kissed her harder instead, gripping tightly to the little bit of sanity he hadn't surrendered.

Her mouth. It was wet and warm, and she tasted like the coffee she'd sipped as they'd traveled, tasted, too, like a feverish panic and…fear. When he slowed the kiss, softening the pressure of his mouth, pulling back, she trembled and moved her hands to his shoulders to hold on.

"I'm not going anywhere, Jamie." He whispered the words against her cheek. "I'm right here. You're safe."

"Safe's not exactly what I'm feeling," she said, and tried to laugh, releasing her grip as if knowing he was close enough for now.

"If you're feeling what I'm feeling…" He watched as she buttoned her shirt, her skin flushed, her fingers fumbling, her expression as dazed and confused as he was feeling. They were headed down a dangerous road here, with neither one of them in a position to enjoy more than the physical trip…or were they?

Was that the danger he was sensing? An emotional connection neither one of them could have anticipated and braced for?

He gave her a hand as she returned to her seat and belted herself in. He then put the vehicle in gear and pulled out of the lot into traffic. He was so screwed. Sex between them was one thing. The complication of hearts and minds was another. The first he could deal with. The second…not now.

Maneuvering through the streets toward their destination, he did his best to put what had happened out of his mind. When he failed at that as miserably as he had at keeping his distance, he forced himself to visualize the crime scene photos from the murders at the Sonora Nites Diner.

It was what he should have been focusing on all along. His work. The job. Solving the case. Using Jamie to do it.

"Is that where we're going?" she asked, and Kell looked up in time to realize he was about to miss his turn.

He pulled into the parking lot and drove around to the rear of the building. They'd be using an office away from the high-traffic area of the station, one set up to look more like a cozy den with the high-tech recording equipment discreetly mounted on a bookshelf between leather-bound volumes, bronze sculptures and dishes of potpourri.

Glancing over at her as he shifted the SUV into park, he gentled his voice and asked, "Are you ready for this?"

"No." Her voice cold and flat, a mere whisper of

fear, she unbuckled her seat belt, climbed down from the vehicle and slammed the door. And there was nothing gentle in the way she did it at all.

9

THE ROOM REMINDED Jamie of a furniture-store showcase. That, or one of the many therapists' offices she'd seen from the inside over the years. From the framed cowboy art, to the saddle-tan leather overstuffed chairs, the den-size area would've made the perfect setting for a John Wayne western, an episode of *Bonanza,* a book written by Louis L'Amour.

She did her best to imagine that's where she was, in a ranch house on the plains, with cattle penned for branding, hands chewing chaws of tobacco, horses corralled and ready for a ride. The only thing that ruined the fantasy was the big picture window behind the half-drawn blinds. No one had told her it was one-way glass, but she knew it was. Knew, too, that Kell would be on the other side while she went back to a place she'd never expected to revisit.

In the deepest part of herself, she knew she was doing the right thing. Knowing so didn't make the process any easier, but interestingly, having Kell there did. Examining why he made all the difference would mean exposing thoughts that were no one's business, and since she was here to open a vein and bleed for the benefit of strangers, she just accepted his strength without question. She even smiled to herself while she did so, breathing deeply to settle her nerves, and sent him a silent thank-you she hoped his heart could hear.

"Miss Danby? Are you comfortable? There's a quilted lap throw folded on the lower shelf of the table there if you're cold."

"I'm fine, thank you," Jamie said to the female technician who would be observing the session and monitoring the recording equipment. From her seat in the recliner against the back wall, Jamie had a full view of Kell's window and the chair from which the male DPS officer would be conducting the session. A second officer would join them, strictly as an impartial observer.

With a nod, the tech moved to her position, a desk situated off to the side, and the two officers, a Sergeant Jay Ready and a Captain Norm Greenley, entered the room. Once introductions had been made, Ready moved to a chair in the corner, easing the door closed behind him, while Greenley, the hypnotist, signaled to the technician to begin the tapes. He gave Jamie a smile.

About sixty, he was dressed similarly to Kell, in boots and jeans and a western-cut dress shirt of starched khaki. His mustache was thick and as white as his hair, his face ruddy, his skin pocked, a testament to many years spent in the sun. He wore a simple wedding band on his left hand, a hefty gold University of Texas class ring on his right.

When he sat in the other recliner, Jamie found her fingers digging into the armrests of hers, her body stiff, her neck and jaw tight, her head beginning to ache.

Telling herself to relax didn't do a bit of good. Her heart was racing, her skin tingling, her stomach threatening to heave up her coffee-and-muffin breakfast.

Captain Greenley squared one leg over the other, folded back the cover of a legal portfolio and pulled a pen from his shirt pocket. He clicked the end and gave the time and date for the tape. "I'm Captain Norman Greenley with the Texas Department of Public Safety. I'm here in Midland, Texas, at the Texas Rangers Company E headquarters, along with media technician Megan Holly and Sergeant Jay Ready. The purpose of this recording is to document an investigative-hypnosis interview with Miss Jamie Danby of Weldon, Texas, also present. Ranger Sergeant Kellen Harding, of the UCIT, is observing from the adjoining room."

For the next thirty minutes, Captain Greenley engaged Jamie in what he explained was a prehypnosis interview. He stated for the record the few basic facts Kell had told him about the case, and established by questioning Jamie that the two of them had not met prior to today.

She listened intently as he advised her of his training and credentials, making sure she understood that he was certified and authorized to conduct the interview, and doing it all in a kindly, genial manner, his tone what she thought of as grandfatherly, his approach that of a natural storyteller, setting her at ease.

"Have you been hypnotized on any other occasion, Jamie?"

"No," she answered, shaking her head.

"Have you ever seen anyone be hypnotized?"

She laughed softly. "Only on TV and in movies."

Captain Greenley laughed, too. "Believe it or not, those demonstrations are actually responsible for the perceptions, and misconceptions, most people have of hypnosis."

Jamie assumed he was going to explain, but prompted him anyway with a curious "Such as?"

"While under hypnosis, you won't be asleep or unconscious. You won't divulge secrets, and you won't be compelled to tell the truth." He clicked his ballpoint again. "Hypnosis is not sodium pentothal."

"You mean it's not truth serum," Jamie said, pulling her legs comfortably into the seat of the big chair.

"Exactly. You won't get stuck in your hypnotized state, and unless you're already of a mind to do so, you can't be made to do anything foolish."

"Like flap my wings and cluck?"

Again, he nodded, smiling. "In a Vegas show, maybe, but not here."

"The real deal," she said, and wondered what Kell was thinking, if he was grinning in that way he had of making her insides quiver.

"Yes, it is," he said, clicked his pen one more time and jotted down a note. "You also need to know that you may remember additional information about the Sonora Nites Diner murders, but you may not. You will, however, remember everything about the session once I bring you out of hypnosis."

She nodded her understanding, relieved to know no one would think her a failure if her memory didn't return, not so relieved to know she'd remember everything after the fact. Over the years, she'd found solace in her amnesia. She'd hate to lose that tiny comfort even though she knew it was time.

"Now, Jamie. I want you to close your eyes, relax and picture your kitchen at home. Think about it for as long as you need to, then describe to me the visualization."

O…kay. "Well, looking into the kitchen from the living room, there's an exit to the right that leads into the hallway, and the refrigerator sits on the other side of that. There's a small strip of countertop, it's a light oak butcher block, between the fridge and the stove, then another larger section that runs into the corner. On the next wall is a window that looks out over the driveway. The sink and dishwasher are there, then the back door.

"The table butts up against the third wall. It can seat four people if pulled out, but I usually eat alone, so I don't bother." She stopped herself from mentioning that she'd eaten there last night with Kell. Even thinking about that right now was too much. "Against the last wall, the one with the door into the living room, is a desk with drawers and shelves. It's where I pay bills and keep cookbooks, stuff like that. The walls are a buttery yellow, the floor white tile, the cabinets the same light oak as the countertops." She opened her eyes, met Greenley's gaze and shrugged. "I guess that's it."

"Good. Very good." The captain nodded. "While you're under hypnosis and I ask you to describe a scene the way it looks in your mind's eye, that's what I want. A detailed visual account of what you see. Understand?"

"Yes. I understand," she said, exhaling deeply as he handed her a form to read through and sign, giving her voluntary consent to participate in the session for the sole purpose of aiding in the criminal investigation.

That done, Captain Greenley went over what she assumed was a standard cover-your-ass checklist, determining that she was not under the treatment of a psychologist or psychiatrist, suffering from any serious physical ailments, taking any stimulants or sedatives without her physician's consent, or subject to any phobias.

The last one made her laugh, but she answered no, and assured him when he reached the end of the questionnaire that she was not wearing contact lenses either. He finished making his notes, then considered her seriously, his brows lowered, and asked, "Do you know where you are right now?"

"Yes, I'm in the Texas Rangers station in Midland, Texas."

"Who asked you to come here today?"

"Ranger Sergeant Kellen Harding."

"What is your understanding of the purpose for coming here?"

"I'll be hypnotized to see if I can remember anything about the murders at the Sonora Nites Diner that will help Sergeant Harding in his investigation of the case."

Greenley's frown softened. "Before we get started, do you have any questions?"

"No, not really. You've been very thorough."

"Very good. Now, Jamie, using your own words, I want you to review for me what you do remember about that night and the events that occurred, in order, exactly as they happened."

"Where do you want me to start?" she asked,

shifting in her chair, fighting the return of the tension along her spine.

"Wherever you would like," he said, then sat back as if he'd paid for a show.

She told him the same story she'd told anyone who'd ever asked. The time she'd clocked in, how she'd waited tables and manned the register with Julio and Elena while Lacy worked in the kitchen with Kass. She'd told him about the last customer they'd never thought would finish his burger and leave, how he'd taken an hour to read the paper, how Julio and Elena had danced up and down the aisle with their mops and brooms after they'd locked the door behind him.

She told him about Kass hurrying all of them to finish because he wanted to get home to Helen. His wife had made his favorite black-forest cake, and he wanted to sit back with a glass of milk, a huge slice of the chocolate-and-cherry layers, and watch the Celtics NBA game on his VCR. He missed Boston a lot, Kass did.

She told Greenley about it being her turn to run the day's closeout tape on the register while balancing the till and preparing the nightly deposit of cash and checks. The credit-card slips went into a separate bag for Kass's bookkeeper, and Jamie had been sorting them, reaching for a paper clip, when the front door's glass had shattered from a spray of bullets and the killer had walked through.

She'd dropped to the floor, her forehead grazed and bleeding, her shoulder, too. The blood from her head wound had puddled around her profusely, and she'd taken short shallow breaths and held them as long as she could, her eyes closed the whole time. That was all she could remember, and she told Greenley that, too.

What she didn't tell him was how she'd felt then, the fear that had been like icy fingers crawling over her skin, the blood that had trickled into her mouth and tasted of death, fearing she would vomit and the killer would realize she was alive, hearing the screams of her friends, the choking, gurgling sounds Elena made as she died.

Those things she kept to herself because they were the hardest memories, the ones that sat like a crushing weight on her chest until she could no longer breathe and went numb. It was the numbness that she hated. She should suffer unbearably for those who had died; the fact that she couldn't caused an embarrassing guilt.

"Good. Very good," Greenley said again, his tone attentive, respectful, his pen silent as he took notes. He looked up then, and met her gaze, smiling as if they had all the time in the world, as if they were old friends catching up on things that had happened in their lives. He made it easy not to give in to her fears and panic.

"Now, Jamie, I want you to relax. Sit back, get comfortable and close your eyes. Good, just like that," he said when she leaned into the chair and let the cushions swallow her up, the feeling heavenly. "Let the tension drain from your limbs. Let your eyelids grow heavy. Breathe in slowly, exhale. That's it. Very good. Become aware of your arms. Allow them to relax. Your hands, too, and your fingers, one by one. That's right. You're doing just fine. In a moment, I'll ask you to count backward from ten. With each number, you'll become even more calm and relaxed until your mind feels like it's floating on a cotton-ball cloud."

That's exactly how Jamie felt, like she was on a cloud, the sky around her calm and blue. She heard her voice from a distance, counting, "Ten, nine, eight… seven…six…" Then she heard Captain Greenley again, telling her there was a television set in front of her, and it would play the movie of the Sonora Nites Diner murders while she told the story again, just like before, only this time she held a remote that could control the picture, speeding it up or slowing it down or pausing it when she needed a closer look.

She went through the same narrative as before, the captain asking her the occasional question about what she was seeing. She saw things she hadn't mentioned the first time, tiny little things she couldn't imagine were important, but were clear and easy to spot when the replay slowed.

And though she'd expected to feel the need to fast-forward through the worst of that night, the truth was she felt detached with Greenley's calm voice assuring her she was safe. Viewing the gory parts was no worse than watching an episode of *CSI*.

When the killer grew closer, however, her heart gave its first jolt, her breath catching in the constriction of her chest. Captain Greenley calmed her, encouraging her to breathe deeply and relax, to take her time describing the scene from her mind's eye.

Wearing blue jeans with ragged hems, the killer stood over her, smelling like diesel fuel and patchouli, and unzipped the deposit bag before banging the register. Coins rained down and pummeled her, the leather pouch landing in front of her face, the sharp corner of the till glancing off her elbow when he knocked it from the counter.

Cursing in Spanish, he kicked her to move her out of his way, and she saw the bloody heel print he left on the floor Elena had mopped and the Nike swoop on his untied black-and-red shoe. His next step, he slipped in a puddle of soapy mop water, reached out to catch himself on the edge of a table, and she saw the tattoo of a coiled rattler on the inside of his wrist.

Once he was out the door and she'd reached the end of the story, Greenley's questions stopped, and in a voice as soothing as ever, he said, "I'm going to bring you back to the present, Jamie, by counting to five. When I finish, you'll remember all of your refreshed memories, understand? Good. Now, one, two, three, four…five."

Jamie opened her eyes, and saw Captain Greenley's smiling mouth beneath the brush of his mustache. He studied her a moment—or maybe he was just giving her time to orient herself in the present—then asked, "How do you feel?"

"Fine," she said as she scooted to sit on the edge of her chair. "I never realized that I'd opened my eyes while I was on the floor. I thought I'd kept them closed until the police arrived and found us. I thought that's why I didn't remember anything but flashes of colors and sounds."

Greenley spent a few more minutes talking to her, then signed off officially for the tape. He got to his feet, and Jamie did the same.

The technician continued to concentrate on her monitor as Jamie turned to follow the captain, leaving the room where she'd spent the last hour and a half and walking into the one where Kell had been watching the hypnosis session—and was now waiting for her.

10

"I'M SORRY." Jamie knew she had nothing to be sorry for, no reason to apologize. She was just saying the words because she knew Kell was disappointed and she had nothing else to give him to take that away.

"Don't be. What you saw is what you saw," he said, clicking the key fob that unlocked his SUV, then walking to the passenger side and opening her door.

She put her hand on the frame, but turned to him instead of climbing into the seat. "But a tattoo? Who doesn't have a tattoo these days? Finding it, or the artist, will be the proverbial needle in a haystack. So much time has passed, not to mention he could very well have had the ink done in Mexico rather than Texas. And let's not even talk about the population of Hispanic males in the state."

Kell nodded toward her seat, most of his expression hidden in the shadow of his big white hat. "Get in."

She started to obey but stopped, put off by his bossy issuing of orders, even more put off by the fact that she was spinelessly following them. "Where are we going?"

He shook his head, looking off over hers into the distance. "I'm not sure. Back to Weldon, I guess. To take you home."

"Can we eat first?" She wasn't ready to go home, but more than that, she was starving. She'd been too nervous this morning to eat more than her usual muffin, but the bran and the banana were long gone. The coffee, too. "A late lunch or early dinner? Either one will do."

"Sure," he said, and when she still didn't move, wanting more of his attention than his vacant stare, he shook off his distracting thoughts and looked down. One brow went up wryly as he added, "But unless you're in the mood to walk, you'll have to get in."

If she'd known her way around, she might've done just that. Walked to the closest restaurant. Physical motion was the best way she knew to clear her mind and harness useless worry. But she was unfamiliar with Midland, so she gave Kell a small bow and climbed into her seat, wishing she hadn't forgotten her sunglasses. The late-summer sun was blinding as it reflected off the vehicle's bright white hood.

By the time Kell slid behind the wheel, she was belted in and thinking about food, having pushed aside thoughts of the hypnosis for now—or that was the case until she realized he'd made no move to start the engine.

Food slipped from her mind, and she frowned, asking, "Are you okay?"

He let out a sigh that was heavy, but she couldn't interpret what the weight of it meant. He could've been feeling almost anything, and holding it back.

But then he said, "Give me a second here," and she knew something somewhere was very very wrong.

"Is everything okay?"

He nodded, his hands on the wheel as he stared down,

For Busy Women Only!

You deserve it!

Mail this card for your:

- ✓ FREE BOOKS & GIFTS
- ✓ Time-saving quick reads
- ✓ Step-saving home delivery
- ✓ Sanity-saving "just for me" treats

Scratch off the gold circle to see the value of your 2 FREE BOOKS and 2 FREE GIFTS. We will send them to you with no obligation to purchase any books, as explained on the back of this card.

We want to make sure we offer you the best service suited to your needs. Please answer the following question:

About how many NEW paperback fiction books have you purchased in the past 3 months?
❏ 0-2 ❏ 3-6 ❏ 7 or more

351 HDL EZVL 151 HDL EZVW

FIRST NAME	LAST NAME

ADDRESS

APT.	CITY

Visit us online at www.ReaderService.com

STATE /PROV. ZIP/POSTAL CODE

The Reader Service - Here's How It Works:

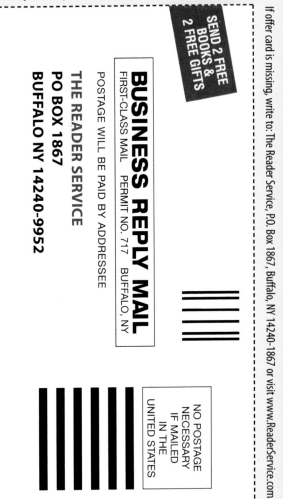

SEND 2 FREE
BOOKS &
2 FREE GIFTS

BUSINESS REPLY MAIL
FIRST-CLASS MAIL   PERMIT NO. 717   BUFFALO, NY

POSTAGE WILL BE PAID BY ADDRESSEE

THE READER SERVICE
PO BOX 1867
BUFFALO NY 14240-9952

NO POSTAGE
NECESSARY
IF MAILED
IN THE
UNITED STATES

his chest rising and falling as if he was struggling to breathe. As if he was fighting down words he wanted to say that she might not want to hear.

Was he angry? Disappointed? Frustrated that she'd recalled so little? Whatever it was, she was now officially worried. "Kell?"

His head came up. "I've read your case file dozens of times. I know from your statement everything that happened that night. But hearing your story in your own words…thinking about you going through that…" A shudder ran through him, seized him. "Jamie, what you just did…"

She waited a moment for him to go on before saying, "It was nothing, Kell. As in literally, nothing. Refreshing my memory didn't net you anything but a tattoo."

"I'm not talking about what you remembered." He turned to face her; his gaze caught hers, held, pulled. "I'm talking about how brave you were to do that. It looked effortless, but I know it wasn't. No way was that easy."

It had seemed easy enough at the time, which surprised her, but mostly she was glad it was over and done. She wasn't feeling haunted, or fearing that she might later suffer nightmares. The whole thing was more like a dream than a return to that horrible night. She started to tell him that.

And then she stopped. He hadn't yet put on his sunglasses, and he was studying her closely, his eyes heated, his lips parted, his jaw held taut against the tic of tension she saw there. Suddenly, all she could think about was what had happened two hours ago, when he'd pulled off the road and into the parking lot and she'd nearly stripped out of her clothes. She wanted to strip out of them now.

She forgot about being hungry, about the hypnosis, about everything except the feel of his mouth and his hands. His touch was a memory she knew she would never need help to recall, and her skin began to burn with wanting him.

Before she could think of all the reasons this was a bad idea, she asked, "Do you live far from here?"

His nostrils flared. He shook his head. Except to reach for the key and turn the ignition, it was his only response. He didn't shift into gear. It was as if he was waiting for permission, wanting to be sure they were on the same page, thinking, craving, the same thing.

Oh, but they were. They were. And she told him so, her heart lodged in her throat, as she softly asked, "Maybe we could go there instead?"

KELL WASN'T GOING TO be able to focus on anything else until he had her. Whether he'd be getting her out of his system by bedding her, or entrenching his desire for her inextricably, he didn't know.

He couldn't know without moving inside of her, without feeling her move beneath him.

She humbled him. He wanted to soak her up and show her more pleasure than she could bear. And it was taking too long to get home.

The drive from the ranger station to his house was one Kell made most every day. Only when away on assignment did he not cover this same stretch of road. Never before had the trip dragged so interminably.

Both the distance and the time were intensified by the impatience eating a hole in his gut. He could smell her, the soft scent of citrus he'd caught on her skin last night.

Was it only last night when she'd crawled all over him in her driveway? Was it only two hours since she'd unbuttoned her blouse in his lap?

He groaned audibly, and he felt her gaze when she looked over. He made the mistake of doing the same, and groaned again when he saw her teething her lower lip, her skin flushed, her eyes wide and dark, the pulse beating in the hollow of her throat synced with his.

He pulled to a stop at a traffic light, sat and stared straight ahead, his blood pressure rising, his body growing stiff. "I didn't plan for this to happen. This isn't something I do."

"What's not something you do? Sex?" she asked, the word sizzling on her tongue.

She'd said it. It was out there. Sex. There was no mistaking where this was going. "I don't…seduce women whose cases I'm working."

"I know," she told him. "That goes against your code. So I'm seducing you instead."

The light changed, and he floored the accelerator, burning rubber into the pavement behind him and feeling like a fool. He was too old to be this desperately horny, but all he could think about was getting his hands on Jamie's ass without her pajama bottoms in the way.

She didn't say anything for the remainder of the drive, but gripped the armrest on her door with one hand, curling the fingers of the other into the denim covering her thigh. He imagined her growing wet for him, and bit off a curse when he took the turn onto his street too fast.

He hit the remote on his visor that opened the garage door, and watched it go up as he pulled into his driveway. Once inside the garage, he shifted into park, shut off the engine and used the remote to send the door back down. And then all he could do was wait.

A curtain of darkness descended, enveloping them and heightening Kell's senses, yet he made no move to leave the SUV. His legs were shaking, his palms sweating, his heart aching, and he could hear Jamie shifting, breathing, kicking off her shoes, getting ready to ease this thing pulsing with a life of its own between them.

The air smelled of heated leather and perfumed skin and hunger, and he couldn't take it anymore. He reached for the telescoping lever and pushed the steering wheel into the dash, reached for the button that controlled his seat and moved it all the way back.

And then, finally—finally!—he turned in the near blackness and reached blindly for her.

She was waiting, and she fell into his arms, her mouth seeking his, her hands finding his shoulders, her fingers digging in and holding on as if she couldn't bear the thought of letting him go.

Her lips were soft, her tongue eager to please. She tasted like sweet desperation, like sex on fire. When he moved his hands from her biceps to the crease where her hips met her thighs, he found skin. Smooth skin. Bare skin. Warm and sleek and taut.

He groaned into her mouth. The sounds he'd heard as she'd scooted around were more than her getting rid of her shoes. But she had yet to get rid of her top, and he wanted her naked more than he wanted to breathe. He started on her buttons while she lifted her hips and straddled him.

He could smell her now. With her thighs parted, he could smell the damp musk of her sex, and he wasn't going to be able to wait, or take this slow, or give her time to catch up. As much as he wanted to seduce her, romance her, his body's demands were much more base.

He needed her now, and once he'd jerked open her blouse, he ordered her to "Raise up."

Their position was awkward, the conditions cramped, but Kell managed to lift his hips, push his pants to his knees, find his wallet and a condom. Once sheathed, he grasped Jamie by the ass and urged her into place, catching his breath when the head of his cock brushed her belly.

While she settled her knees on either side of his hips, he fumbled for the catch that released the seat and laid it flat. Jamie hovered above him, her hands gripping the padded leather on either side of his shoulders, her bent legs pressed tightly to his.

He reached between her thighs with one hand, slid his index finger through her wet folds, parting them, then pushed his middle finger inside her as far as he could. He added a second, and she gasped, then gripped him.

His cock throbbed. His blood heated. He struggled to breathe. His heart beat in a rhythm that further constricted a chest already tight with emotion. It was a rhythm brought on by this thing with Jamie. This thing that was more than sex. A more he didn't know what to do with yet. A more he wasn't sure his life was ready for.

His free arm across her back urged her down, and he found a nipple with his tongue and drew it into his mouth, rolling it and latching on. This he could do. This he knew how to enjoy, to savor, to give. He sucked on her, he fingered her. He smiled against her when she squirmed.

And when she begged, "Kell, please," he let her go, held her hips, and guided her body into place above his. She lowered herself slowly, found the head of his cock, opened for him and slid all the way down. Then she sat, stilled, did nothing but squeeze him with her muscles inside.

This time, he was the one to beg. "Jamie, don't."

She leaned over him, planting her elbows and forearms on the seat above his shoulders, her mouth hovering inches from his as she began to move. She lifted her hips until only the head of his cock was inside her. She lowered her sex until she'd swallowed the length of his shaft. She gyrated in a slow figure eight. She pumped up and down in piston-like strokes, fast, then slow, then slower. She made love to him as if she wanted to make sure he'd never forget.

As if that would ever happen. Kell swore he was going to die before he got a chance to come. He clenched the muscles of his legs, crunched his abs and grabbed Jamie where her ass met her thighs, pulling them open, thrusting up and burying himself all the way to his balls.

She kissed him then, covered his mouth with hers and sent her tongue seeking, her lips nibbling, her teeth nipping. She kissed him like kissing was the best part of sex, and he wasn't sure he could disagree. She let him into her mouth, giving him that pleasure as she gave him her body. He was ripe with waiting and ready to burst.

He pulled his mouth away, needing it to breathe, and drove himself into her again and again. She rested her forehead on his, breathing just as hard as he was, breathing his air, breathing him in and riding him, up and down, meeting his strokes.

And then she came, arching up and crying out as if the sudden rush of sensation caught her unawares, drowning her, sucking her into the same whirlwind that had tightened around him and squeezed.

That was it. He was done. One last thrust and he let everything go, feeling as if he were being turned inside out with each pulse of semen he shot. He grunted. It was the only sound he could make, the only sound that fit with the primal urge he had to own her.

She collapsed against him, her breasts flat on his chest, her face in the crook of his neck and shoulder. He wrapped her up in his arms and held her there, still connected, cocooned safely together in the darkness, thinking it might just be a very long time before either of them wanted to move.

_11_

By the time Jamie finished pulling herself together in Kell's bathroom, he'd whipped up a huge lunch of bacon, lettuce, tomato, onion and cheese sandwiches, with tomato soup and Cheetos. Bachelor fare. Because he was a bachelor. A confirmed one at that.

She was surprised at his house, the very Martha Stewart decor. She wondered if his mother had decorated the place because she'd visited and found him living out of boxes or with dorm-room furniture or even with no furnishings at all.

Then she wondered how long he'd lived here, how many women he'd brought home to share his bed. She didn't know why she was wondering that; it was none of her business, and this strange sense of possessiveness stirring her made little sense. It wasn't as if they'd exchanged vows while in the garage.

The bathroom Kell had pointed her to when they'd finally made it inside had perfumed soaps and guest towels and nothing to indicate the shower had ever seen use. She'd thought at first he might join her. She had almost asked him to.

He'd hesitated in the doorway as if he wasn't ready

to walk away, or to let her out of his sight, or to lose her. His belt had been hanging loose, his crisp white shirt untucked, his expression as rumpled and used as the rest of him, uncertain, spent. But then he'd backed away, and told her he'd clean up in the master bath. Said for her to take her time, he'd have their very late lunch ready when she was.

And so she hadn't said anything, just nodded and closed the door, leaning against it and shutting her eyes, hoping to calm the rush of blood through her veins and catch her breath. She'd tied up her hair and stayed beneath the warm spray for twenty minutes. But her legs were still shaking when she followed the smell of the food to the kitchen and found him setting the table for two.

Soupspoons in hand, Kell looked up. He was freshly shaven, his skin glowing, his hair still damp and sticking up here and there. As usual, he had on jeans, but he was barefoot instead of in boots, and wearing a faded maroon Texas A&M T-shirt that showed off his shoulders and arms in ways his dress shirts never could.

He straightened and smiled, stopping what he was doing to stare at her as she stood in the doorway. The moment went on too long, the silence, the snap, crackle, pop of tension in the air, and he cleared his throat, saying, "I wasn't sure what you'd like. If you're not into bacon, I've got turkey. Or chicken noodle soup instead of the tomato."

"The tomato is fine. The bacon is fine. And I love Cheetos more than any other chip." She came farther into the room, pushed from behind by urgency, feeling the sizzle between them nipping at her skin. She wasn't sure if she should sit, or help, or get drinks…

"Do you want me to—"

"I'm sorry. I shouldn't have—"

"Don't be sorry. I was just as much—"

"Waiting was just too hard—"

"I know. It was. It still is. I want—"

"You want? What? Tell me—"

"To eat?" she ended with because otherwise they were going to linger here forever, wanting each other, and starve.

"Yeah," he said, dipping his head with a small laugh. "That's probably a good idea."

Jamie took a big breath, felt better when she blew it out and most of the stress she'd been holding in with it. She padded the rest of the way across the cool red brick tiles to the circular table and the chair Kell had pulled out for her.

He sat in the chair to her right. There was enough distance between them that neither their arms nor their thighs brushed, but she still felt the heat of his body, the pull of his nearness, the draw. It was hard not to remember the way he'd touched her, the way he'd filled her. He'd been so thick and full, and he'd reached so deep.

She tamped down a rising flood of desire and forced her trembling hand to still before picking up her spoon. She couldn't, however, stop herself from clenching the muscles of her sex. God, but she wanted him again. "This all smells so good. Thank you."

"It's soup and sandwiches. Took all of ten minutes to throw together," he said, but then when he noticed the arch of her brow, added, "You're welcome."

"That's better. It may be just soup and sandwiches, but you prepared it, and all I have to do is eat." She dipped up a spoonful of soup, blew softly across the surface, and before she ate, added, "And that makes me very happy."

"Good. I like making you happy," he came back with, and she thought she was going to choke.

She took a minute to clear her throat. "So far, you've done just about everything right. But then, in case you haven't noticed, I'm not hard to please."

This time he was the one who almost spit sandwich crumbs everywhere. He got up and grabbed two bottles of water from the fridge, handed her one and gulped down a big swallow of his before responding. "I guess there's something to be said for low maintenance."

"Exactly." She set down her spoon, popped back a Cheeto and chewed. "If I were high maintenance, I'd prefer a pomegranate cocktail to the Jim Beam, a salad of arugula and mixed greens to the Cheetos, and Egyptian cotton to GMC's leather beneath my knees."

He tensed, lifted his spoon and let it hover over his bowl. "I don't think you have to be high maintenance to prefer soft sheets to a truck seat."

He stopped, though she could tell he had more to say. She prompted him to go on. "But?"

He set down his spoon, rested his wrists on the table's edge, stared down at his food. "I'm just wondering if you being easy to please means you won't slap me silly when I tell you I really don't want to eat."

Oh. My. It was a struggle to find her voice, what with the way her heart was lodged in her throat. "Why don't you tell me and find out."

"I want to take you to bed." He looked up and met her gaze; his was hungry, unsatisfied and frighteningly dark. As if having her in the truck hadn't been enough of a taste of all the things he wanted to know and to feel, to learn of her. "Now."

She licked her lips, wanting the same thing, wondering if she'd be smart to resist, or if giving in would be enough to get him out of her system so she wouldn't miss him after he took her home and left her there.

Because that was her biggest fear, that when she looked back on today, it wouldn't be the hypnosis that scared her, but the thought of what she'd missed out on with Kell. She slid her palms down her thighs and told him without flinching, "I'd like it very much if you did."

He got to his feet, held out his hand. She laid her fingers on his palm, and he closed his over them, tugging until she, too, stood. Still, he didn't say anything. She watched the muscles in his throat work as he swallowed, watched the tic of his pulse in his temple as his blood surged. She wondered if he could see similar signs in her, signs of wanting and impatience and need. Tingles tightened the skin over her chest, like tiny electric charges shocking her.

Kell nudged away their chairs, and she thought briefly that they should cover the sandwiches so the bread wouldn't grow stale, the bacon cold, the vegetables warm. Thought, too, about returning the soup to the pan, the caps to the bottles of water. Then she thought about nothing more than following Kell to his bedroom.

The food could wait. The things she wanted from him had waited too long already. Whatever happened after today, she was through putting her life on hold, and if nothing else, she'd have him to thank for that.

His bedroom might have been decorated originally by the same person who had put Martha Stewart's touch on the rest of his place, but he'd put his own mark on the room since. It was lived in, a man's room, but not a pizza-box, beer-can, dirty-clothes pigsty. Just cluttered with his things.

Boots and athletic shoes and copies of *Time* and *Wired*. T-shirts were rolled, rather than folded, and piled on top of his chest of drawers as if he hadn't had time to put them away. Socks, too. Not matched or bunched into pairs, but dropped into a clothes basket with clean boxer shorts.

His furniture was the color of pecan, the pieces large, his curtains and duvet an abstract geometric pattern in shades of rawhide and rust. He had a bookshelf filled with paperbacks, jug lamps with wide-bottomed shades and a single framed print of a cattle drive she knew was a Frederic Remington.

There was no TV, and for some reason that surprised her. It occurred to her to ask if he read himself to sleep, but he stopped at the foot of the bed, and once there, turned to face her. "Look at me, Jamie."

She took a deep breath, eased it out and lifted her gaze. It was the hardest thing she'd ever done. Sex in the garage had been easy. The darkness had been the perfect shield, hiding her physical flaws, her huge case of nerves, masking all the things she knew his eyes would say if she could see them.

She couldn't escape any of that now, though the flaws

and the nerves were nothing when compared to the impact of standing so near, face-to-face, both of them barefoot, and remembering the feel of their joining, of being one. Of knowing a return to that pleasure was as close as his bed.

He brought his free hand to her cheek, stroked a thumb along the ridge of her cheekbone, tucked his fingertips behind her ear and made her shiver. Then he lifted the hand he was holding and pressed her palm to his chest.

"Feel that?"

His heart. It was wild, a flock of birds beating their wings on liftoff, horses' hooves pounding across the wide-open range. The wind, powering through tree boughs, whitecapping once-calm waves. She nodded, breathed, "Yes."

"It's been doing this since I walked into your office yesterday. I can't make it stop."

Smiling, she widened the spread of her fingers. His muscles beneath her hand were taut, firm, his flesh resilient. "I don't think you want it to stop. That would mean you were dead. And I would like you alive for a little while longer. Until I get my fill at least."

He slid his palm down the side of her neck to her shoulder. "Any idea how long that will take? Because I'll need to schedule recovery time. I have a feeling you're going to wear me out."

"You can tell that already?" She moved both of her hands over his rib cage and settled them at his waist, cocking her head to the side. "After only one time?"

He reached for the hem of his T-shirt, pulled the garment over his head and let it fall to the carpet. Then he waited until she was touching him again, her hands back at his waist, his skin burning, before he went on. "I knew what you'd be like before I had you. It's there in your eyes, in what you say, what you think and do. It was there last night in your driveway."

"I wanted you last night. It wasn't the JB. It wasn't the moon. It wasn't fear. It was me. I wanted you."

"I know," he told her, reaching for the buttons down the front of her blouse, pulling it off and dropping it. Then he reached for the buttons of her fly.

"But you put me off." She kicked out of her jeans.

He shook his head, then leaned close, soothing her with tiny kisses to her collarbone, his fingers molding her breasts. "We needed today out of the way. And barely managed that."

She shivered, her nipples tightening, the stirring in her belly now nothing but desire, anticipation, a ready-ing of her sex. She knew how he fit, and she wanted him there, and found her hands cupping his erection where it strained.

"Not yet," he said, winding their legs like braided strands and backing her into the mattress. Her knees hit, and he lowered her, then left her, taking her panties with him and kneeling at her feet.

She closed her eyes, chilled by the ceiling fan circu-lating the air, but oh, the heat between her legs. Kell had spread her knees, exposing her sex, and was licking and kissing and biting his way the length of her inner thighs. His mouth was hot, his lips and tongue sure, his teeth sharp enough to sting. She loved it. She wanted more, and curled her fingers into the duvet to hold on.

A butterfly. Tickling, flitting, brushing air as it fluttered its wings. That's what Kell's mouth felt like when he reached her sex. He licked her, wet her, blew warm breath to bring her to life, and then he caught her clit with his lips and tugged.

She arched into him, her hips and pelvis coming up off the bed. Oh, he was good as he worked her with his mouth, slipping a finger inside of her to thrust. He knew what he was doing, and she was so close to the edge that she almost let go, but even more than coming again, she wanted to have him with her when she did.

Bringing her heels to her hips, she used her feet to push herself farther up the bed. She wanted him to cover her, she wanted to feel his heaviness, she wanted to have all of him naked, not just his mouth and his hands and his cock. And without her having to ask, he followed, standing first to shuck out of his boxers and jeans.

Their eyes met and held as he crawled over her on his hands and knees, resting his weight on his forearms above her shoulders, and lowering his chest, then his belly, then his hips to align with hers. Though she was half his weight, she welcomed the feel of his body pressing hers into the mattress, because for reasons she didn't want to stop and examine, he kept the outside world and its threats at bay.

The thought should have made her smile. It sobered her instead. And whatever change came over her expression as she realized the true danger she was facing, Kell saw it and stopped.

12

"THIS ISN'T WHAT you want?" Kell wasn't sure if he was making a statement or asking a question. He did know there was something wrong here. That wherever they'd been moments ago, the world had shifted and dumped them in a place where he'd yet to find his footing. He was hard, and wanting, and feeling rejected. This wasn't good.

"Oh, no," she said, holding on to his arms. "Don't think that. Please, this *is* what I want."

She was shaking her head where it rested on the bed between his arms, and he thought she was reassuring him that things were okay, but the sliver of what looked like uncertainty, maybe even regret, left him hanging.

He couldn't do this if she wasn't sure. "Jamie, what's wrong?"

She squeezed shut her eyes, and when she pulled in a breath, it caught as a sob she couldn't laugh away. "I'm sorry. This is so humiliating."

For her or for him? He rolled to the side, left one leg on top of hers to keep her beside him. He wasn't going to let her get away until he knew why she was falling apart.

And then it hit him, the things she'd been through today,

the things she'd relived and remembered. Her emotions had to be ragged, and all he could think of was rutting.

He was a toad. "Are you cold?"

She wiped her eyes. "I'm fine, really. I don't even know what happened. I was thinking about being in danger, and you making me feel safe."

Yeah. Not a good thing. "And that made you cry?"

She tried to laugh, managed what came out sounding like a hiccup, covered her mouth and turned her head, their gazes connecting. "If I tell you the truth will you promise not to run away scared?"

Why would he run away scared? "I promise not to run away, but I can't promise not to worry."

She stroked her thumb over his mouth, then rolled onto her side to face him. They were so close that her nipples brushed against his chest when either of them breathed.

"You don't need to worry about anything," she said. "I'm not going to fall apart on you, more than I already have, anyway. Or try to trap you into a relationship just because we've slept together."

Now he was simply confused. Was she crying because she wanted a relationship, or because she didn't? "You trying to trap me hasn't crossed my mind even once."

"Good, because that's not who I am." She wedged both of her arms between them, plucked at his chest hair with her fingers, twisted her mouth to one side as if trying on the fit of her next words. "It's just…"

That was all she got out before she started twisting again, plucking again, plucking harder. He grabbed her busy fingers, kissed their tips, then held them still instead of transferring them to the part of his body that, even softened, ached for her touch. "It's just what, Jamie? You feel this is a mistake?"

She frowned, and cuddled even closer to him, her lips grazing the skin just this side of his armpit. "Why would you think that?"

"I don't think that, but when a woman starts crying on me in bed…"

"I accepted a long time ago that I was going to live my life alone." She pushed out the words in a rush, as if it was the only way she could let them go. "I've tried on a few men, found them comfortable enough, but none of them were men I could see myself still wearing at the end of my life."

A strange dressing-room metaphor, but he got it. He'd decided to remain a bachelor for much the same reason. Dates offered him company and conversation, and occasionally the chance to share his release instead of flying solo in the shower at the end of the day. But sex wasn't a relationship. At least not the sex he'd had before.

And that was the problem here, wasn't it? What he and Jamie had going on was more than physical involvement. "So you don't want me to run away scared because I feel like I could turn into an old shoe. Is that it?"

She giggled as if picturing a funny image. But then she sighed, growing pensive again. "That's part of it, yes. But the other part is knowing that after this, we're going to get up and dress, and hopefully eat, and then you'll be taking me home. You might touch base every few months to keep me posted on the investigation, but that's it. I'm never going to get the chance to break you in. I feel like I finally found the buy of a lifetime, and the store closed its doors before I could get inside."

Because she'd seen the same potential between them that he had. Because she'd quit the idea of exploring it before starting the climb. He had, too. Neither of them wanted to risk screwing up their perfectly good lives. But both feared the real screwup would be in letting this go.

What to do? "You really know how to make a guy feel like a bargain. And how to stretch a metaphor."

"Hey, at least I didn't compare you to a piece of meat," she said, and winked, winding her legs in and out of his. "Thank you for not running away. For letting me spill all of that."

"Is that it, then?" he asked, though he knew "it" was a whole lot more complicated than getting things out in the open. They were still there to be dealt with. "You stopped me from finishing what I started because of your shopping woes?"

"I was overwhelmed." She draped one arm around his waist, slid her hand lower, spread her fingers over the cheek of his ass and nuzzled her nose to his throat. "Since living in Weldon, I haven't done much shopping. It can take a lot out of a girl."

She'd been living in Weldon ten years. A waste of so much time she could have been doing whatever twenty-somethings were doing then. But he couldn't think about that now, not when her fingers were walking into places he'd never before allowed anyone access. "I've got something to put in you, if you think it'll help."

"I think you're exactly what I need right now." That

was all she said as she urged his lower body closer with the press of her hand to his hip.

The thought of a future with many such days spent in bed beside her… As he rolled on top of her and lowered himself into her welcoming cradle, Kell forced the thought from his mind. They were here together now, and he didn't want their shared longing for anything else getting in the way of making this memory unforgettable.

Threading his fingers into her hair, he held her still for his kiss, blinding himself to all sensation but that of her mouth. His tongue found hers waiting, eager to please, found it bold. They pressed against each other, rocking, seeking, her lips tugging at his to keep him from moving away.

He moved anyway, kissed her jaw, her neck, from her shoulder to her collarbone to the hollow of her throat. To her breasts. She kneaded his biceps and kept him there, pulling him up her body when he tried to go down. He smiled against her skin, then returned to nuzzle his face to hers as he slid his sheathed cock inside her.

When he hit bottom, he stopped, feeling her tighten around him, feeling her shudder, still and release. She pulled her hips away, withdrawing to make him follow, pushing down into the mattress, and he did. He didn't want to lose the feel of being cloaked within her, of being lost inside her, of being one, and he surged deeper.

Jamie gasped, and he wanted to kick himself for not thinking of her comfort, focused only on the things he craved, but then she shifted, tilting her hips to accommodate him more fully.

And then she whispered hoarsely, "Give me more."

He laughed, growled, a deep gravelly noise that felt as rough in his chest as it sounded in the air. "How much of me do you want?"

"How much you got?" she came back with, digging her heels into his rump and holding him tightly in place.

It was no longer a question. In this woman, he had met his match. He crawled farther up her body. "How much do you think you can take?"

She arched her back, ground her clit against the base of his shaft, her hips rolling beneath him and drawing shuddering groans from them both. "I think we'd better just stick to the sex."

He laughed again, this time as a cover-up, because knowing it was too late for just sex, he was going to lie. "That I can do."

"Then do it," she told him.

With his forearms above her shoulders bearing the bulk of his weight, he began to stroke, his mind on what his body was doing, his thoughts centered on his cock, on her sex, his concentration on nothing but physical pleasure. Or so he told himself as he drove deeper, harder, pumping long and slow, a piston firing, sparking to life.

Her breathing told him how close she was, and he moved where she told him to with a nudge of her knee, a bump from her fist, a bucking up of her lower body into his. She made sounds, anxious sounds, moans of desperation, mindless huffs and grunts, squeaks of impatience as she reached for the end.

She found it, crying out as she came, her head and shoulders pushing into the bed, her chin lifting. He watched her face; tension drained in a rush, and the smile that followed sent him over the edge. His orgasm ripped through him, a blast of sensation that staggered him, pulsing waves that flattened him. Even his knees betrayed him. He collapsed like a rag doll, spilling himself in a flood.

Jamie held his weight, held him, soothing him with her hands that rubbed his back and shoulders, quieting him and bringing him back with her voice that whispered, "Shh," over and over again.

As if he had the energy to speak, the brain to search out coherent thought, the need to say anything besides words of emotion he knew were best left silenced. For now, anyway. Telling her what he was feeling while her body still claimed his was cliché. Sex talk. Heat of the moment. Endorphins tickling his tongue. Not truth.

He wasn't ready for the truth. The truth scared him. He'd known since childhood what he wanted to do with his life. He accepted that chasing bad guys brought him into harm's way more often than he liked.

He'd decided that was a risk he was willing to take, but not one he was sure was fair to ask a partner, a lover, a wife, to take on. He wasn't going to give up his calling, so he'd given up hoping to share his life.

He came with a lot of heavy baggage, though that wouldn't stop him from taking on the baggage of someone he loved. He'd just never thought he'd find someone in similar circumstances, a partner, a soul mate, someone who understood, who could take on all his baggage in return.

And so it scared him to think that he had. In Jamie.

13

WHEN JAMIE AND KELL finally left his house, the sun was long set, the street lamps shining down along with the light of the moon. Jamie wanted to stand in Kell's driveway and wrap herself up in him as she'd done only twenty-four hours ago in hers. Only twenty-four hours? Could it be?

And all that had happened in it. The way she'd climbed over him naked in his garage, in the dark, in the seat of his SUV. The way he'd fed her, cared for her, listened to her fears, and loved her as if…as if he meant it.

He didn't. He couldn't. She knew that. He was her Texas Ranger and she was his case. More fraternization than they'd already engaged in was asking for more trouble than they were already in. And she was pretty sure that they were in a lot. A very big lot.

With his SUV idling beside her, she stood watching his garage door slide closed, then climbed up in the passenger seat of the vehicle. He'd been sitting there waiting, the engine running. She'd had to talk herself into going home. Being here with Kell…she felt closer than she had in years to Stephanie Monroe.

And how weird was that? she mused, buckling her

shoulder strap into place. She'd made her life in Weldon, had felt safe in Weldon, knew the lay of the land there, the people in town.

Was that the problem? As much as she loved her home, was it more the place she'd run to escape her past? More a prison instead of a harbor? Being with Kell made her feel safe, secure, as if she belonged, instead of as if she'd had to forge a good fit. This was strange, wrong, so very—

"Shit!" Kell slammed on his brakes, adding, "Sorry, sorry," when she surged forward and choked on her shoulder strap. "I almost backed into that car. Across the street. I knew I'd cleared the mailbox, but…shit. Sorry. Guess the Feagans have guests."

He shifted from Reverse into Drive and they traveled toward the intersection. There they stopped, and Kell readied to turn. Jamie checked her side mirror, and saw the car's headlights come on before it pulled away from the curb.

Her nape tingled. "Would their guests be waiting for any reason for you to leave?"

"What?" Kell looked into his rearview and saw the car approach. "Hmm" was all he said as he made his turn, watching to see if the car followed. It didn't, heading in the opposite direction. Still, Jamie couldn't look away, staring until the car's taillights vanished.

So much for feeling safe. Suddenly, the reason for her being in Midland to begin with came rushing back, and she wished they were returning to Weldon in broad daylight, not in the dark of night that made her think too much about the memories refreshed during hypnosis.

Maybe if she talked it out? "Once you drop me off

and get back to work tomorrow, what's your first step? On the case? Assuming you don't have new evidence come in on another. Since I gave you nothing to work with on this one."

He reached across the console and took hold of her hand. "I'm not writing off this case just because the hypnosis didn't give us as much as I'd hoped."

"As much? It didn't give you anything." A tattoo. A Nike swoop. Orders issued in Spanish, a language she had a better grasp of now than she did then, but not enough of one to make sense of what the killer had said.

There were more Hispanic men in this part of Texas than there were Caucasian, and all she'd seen of the killer was his wrist, the ragged hem of his jeans and the shoes that had left bloody footprints on the diner's freshly mopped floor.

She closed her eyes, leaning her head back against the seat. "I wanted so badly to give you the answers you needed."

"Jamie, listen to me. What you gave the investigation was exactly what it needed. You gave it the details of what you saw. You can't be faulted for not seeing more than you did. God, woman." He squeezed her fingers. "The fact that you had enough in the way of wits to see that much is nothing short of amazing."

"You're just being nice." She wished she could believe him, but she felt like a failure. She'd failed Kell, herself, her friends who'd lost their lives that night.

"You're right. I am nice, but that's not what I'm doing."

"What are you doing?" Because, if he had a magic answer, she wanted to know.

"I'm telling you how I really feel. About the outcome of the hypnosis. About how you've handled living with this all these years. I don't think I've known another woman as brave as you are."

"Is that 'known' in the biblical sense?"

"No," he said, and laughed. "Though I'd include those in the total."

"What about your mother? She raised three boys." She paused, pictured Kell as the oldest of three adolescent males running through the Harding family home. It made her smile, and she bounced their joined hands on her thigh. "A woman would have to be brave to take on more than one like you."

"My mother is brave, but trust me when I say I gave her and my dad less hell than my brothers combined."

"What, were you the perfect son? Bossing your brothers around? Ruling the sibling roost with an iron fist?"

"Something like that," he said, pulling his hand from hers to turn the steering wheel. She tried not to feel bereft, but the contact made such a difference, so she reached across and laid her hand on his thigh.

Kell went on. "I was six when Brennan was born, and Terry came along the next year. The two of them being so close in age was like having twin heathens running wild. As they got older, they looked to me, rather than to our parents, for answers, like having been there already, I would know what they could get away with before someone with real authority put down a foot."

Cute. A mini Texas Ranger, ordering the younger two boys to stand at attention. She could imagine the respect and admiration shining in their eyes. "You were their role model."

"I guess so," he said, shrugging as he guided the SUV onto the highway that would take them back to Weldon.

The man was too modest, but then, she liked that about him, the way he saw no need for braggadocio, machismo. He was a man secure in who he was, the best sort. "What do you mean guess? A big brother who knew the lay of the land? Whose parents afforded him extra privileges and responsibility because he'd earned them?"

He chuckled. "Assuming a lot there, aren't you?"

She was, but she knew she was right. "Am I wrong? Were you not a younger version back then of who you are now?"

"Yeah, I had a thing about rights and wrongs. I stood up for more than one bullied kid in school. Also lost some friends because I wouldn't go along with their pranks. Papering houses was about as criminal as I ever got." He checked his mirrors, changed lanes, set the cruise control and got comfortable. "I wanted to play ball, have the respect of my coaches and team, and not have my college admission threatened by the stupid stuff teens do. Not sure if that made me a wet blanket or a Goody Two-shoes."

"I'd say it made you perfect for what you do." Surely he saw that. "There are lots of people who like to straddle the line between right and wrong, to see what they can get away with, or pull off as long as no one gets hurt."

"But that's the thing," he said, launching into something she could tell he felt passionately about. "Someone always gets hurt. Pranks, pyramid schemes, public intoxication, whatever. There's always a victim. Even if it's just the sanitation worker hosing away the drunk's vomit. Or the guy who has to clean the damp toilet paper out of his yard the next morning."

Huh. He'd kept that memory with him for a while. She shifted in her seat to better see him, the amber lights from the dash catching his jaw, his cheekbones. "You went back and helped, didn't you?"

"Went back?"

"And helped him with the toilet paper. You drove by on your way to school or football practice, saw the unholy mess, and your conscience made you stop."

He snorted. "Like I said. Goody-Two shoes."

"No, Kell Harding. You're a good man," she said, and meant it more than he could ever know.

He, of course, had to share the credit for his becoming the man he was. "I had a couple of role models of my own."

"Your father, and who else?" she asked, letting her eyes drift shut. She was beyond exhausted. The sex, the hypnosis, the identification of Kass's body, her cold case once again hot… It was amazing she hadn't fallen asleep while she and Kell ate their reheated food.

"Captain Warren Sheets," he told her. "My first supervisor as a Ranger, and a longtime friend of my father's. He convinced me to go into law enforcement just by being the man that he was. Respectful as well as respected. Upstanding and honest. A man you could count on."

Warren Sheets. It sounded so familiar. "I know that name. Why do I know that name?"

Kell paused, letting the question hang several seconds

before answering. "He was the original investigator on the Sonora Nites Diner case."

Jamie's eyes popped open. Her heart blipped, and she was suddenly wide, wide awake. "Oh my God. He was. But you didn't work it then, did you? I don't remember you being there at any of the interviews."

Kell shook his head. "Not officially, though I spent a lot of late hours with Warren combing through evidence."

"So when you said you were familiar with the case—"

"I wasn't kidding. Finding the killer has been a personal crusade, I guess you could say. Warren swore to see the man behind bars if it was the last thing he did. The crime scene…it really got to him. All the years I knew him, he never could let it go. The department might've called the case cold, but Warren—" Kell shook his head "—he never did. He died with this case still haunting him."

And Kell had sworn to finish his mentor's work, Jamie realized, realizing, too, that he had his own stake in this case, one driving him that had nothing to do with her. For the first time she wondered how this thing between them would impact him doing his job.

Would he make choices he might not have made otherwise? Would it be harder for him to put it away if it grew cold again? Would he suffer more guilt should he not be able to close it because of what they'd shared? Would she always wonder if this interlude had been, for Kell, a professional misstep?

God, her head hurt from thinking of all the ramifications of what they'd done. "You've taken up where he left off, then."

"I'm doing my job, Jamie," he reiterated. "If Kass Duren's body hadn't been found and identified, I'd be working on whatever case had the newest leads. It might've been this one, it might've been another."

It sounded good. She just had trouble buying it. He'd said Warren Sheets had influenced his life as greatly as his father. Finishing what the other man had started would be more than a job. It would be a calling. A vow.

"Why don't I believe that?" she asked softly.

He huffed once, twice, then cursed under his breath, the words self-directed, not meant for her. "Because somehow you've learned to read my mind? Or at least read me?"

"At the very least," she told him, because even *she* hadn't yet figured out the depth of their involvement.

"I used to be better at keeping my mouth shut."

"With women, or in general?" she heard herself asking.

He gave her another of his laughs that she loved hearing, then sighed. "Always back to the women with you, isn't it?"

She felt as if she had a vested interest in him now. And with the Weldon city limits looming, her time with him was too swiftly coming to an end. She wasn't ready to lose him.

She wasn't ready to let go. "You're staying over, aren't you? You're not driving back to Midland tonight?"

They hadn't talked about their parting, whether he'd drop her off at her front door, or tell her goodbye in the morning. They hadn't talked about keeping in touch, whether he'd check in with her on a regular basis, or if she should just wait for his updates as they came.

They hadn't talked about the end at all. Did that mean neither one of them wanted it to come?

Finally, Kell broke the silence that was eating her alive. "If you want me to stay, I'll stay."

Oh, she did, she did, but… She twisted her fingers together; she didn't want to reach for him too soon. "Only if that's what you want."

He leaned over, settled his hand at her nape, threaded his fingers into her hair and kneaded her there. Tingles of longing tightened her breasts. "I want it more than anything."

14

WHEN JAMIE HAD PURCHASED her cottage and moved out of the house she'd shared with her mother their first five years in Weldon, she'd also bought the four-poster bed she'd dreamed of since seeing it in a home-decor magazine as a teen.

It was a simple wrought-iron frame in matte black, the canopy draped with sheer white lace panels that made her think of harem curtains, umbrellas with privacy veils, tinted windows—all hinting at the secrets being kept behind.

Waking up along with the dawn and beside a sleeping Kell, Jamie realized her canopied bed now held secrets of its own—secrets she would keep close, share with no one, relishing them in private when life left her lonely.

Sure, she would fill her days with work, and have her mother, her friends and neighbors for company. And she would not feel sorry for herself, embracing instead every moment of joy that came her way, even creating them. But this time with Kell would never be far from her mind.

Their paths had crossed on this one particular road, but wishing for more would be folly. His knowing about her past didn't mean he wanted to live with it, to have to face down her ghosts when they drifted in, unannounced and unexpected, to haunt her.

Still, she'd be forever grateful for the way he'd helped her connect to lost pieces of Stephanie, for the way he'd helped her find the answers to the lingering questions about the night of the murders.

And he'd given her so much more…laughter and deep conversation, tenderness and fiery passion, honesty and hard truths. With every fiber of who she was, she knew she would never get the same from any other man.

She turned onto her side to watch him. He lay beside her on his back, the sheet she clutched beneath her chin draped across his torso, leaving his chest bare. One of his arms rested on top of the bedclothes between them. The other hand was spread low on his belly.

He wasn't a cuddler, she'd discovered, and that was okay. Just knowing he was there during the night had made her dreams serene, and every once in a while when she'd adjusted her position, she'd brushed up against him, her knee, her heel, her fingers when she'd stretched, and she'd roused enough to smile, somewhere between wakefulness and sleep.

Now that she was awake, she refused to allow herself to drift off again and miss any more of this time. She wanted to move closer to him, to enjoy his warmth, his weight sinking into the mattress, his bulk beside her lifting the sheet when she was so used to it lying flat around her.

She scooted toward him, quietly, an inch at a time, doing her best not to rock the frame or pull the covers. She watched his chest rise and fall, felt the heat of his body as she drew near, and then he moved the arm blocking her way, and mumbled, "I'm awake, you know."

"I know," she whispered back, though she hadn't been certain.

"Hard to sleep with you thinking so hard over there."

She laughed to herself, a soft sound that came out on her next breath. At least he couldn't hear *what* she was thinking. She didn't want to scare him away.

"It's okay," he mumbled. "I'm not going to shoo you off and roll over."

Or could he hear it all? His eyes were still closed, his lips barely parted. His cheeks were covered with a dark shadow of beard, and she liked this scruffy, disheveled Kell as much as the clean and pressed Texas Ranger version. "I didn't want to disturb you."

He peered at her through one slitted lid. "Too late. I'm disturbed."

A tingling set up in the pit of her belly. "Maybe I'll just stay where I am—"

"Don't even think about it," he said, and reached for her, tugging the sheet out of the way as she climbed on top and straddled him. "My disturbance needs attention."

So she'd noticed. "A trip to the facilities maybe?"

"I made one an hour ago," he grumbled. "This is all you."

Hmm. She hadn't even heard him get out of bed. "Feels to me like it's all you."

"Then you're obviously not doing enough feeling."

She was feeling with her inner thighs, with her belly. The head of his cock pushed there, hot, sticky with the moisture of his arousal. She knew this would be their last time, and she didn't want to rush through loving him.

The sheet was white and cool on her back, a contrast to the warmth and dark hair she encountered along her front as she moved down his body to take him into her mouth. He exhaled, a long slow potent groan that thrilled her, rumbling beneath her, a rocky surface, as it did.

He tasted like rich wine and salt and dark earthy musk, and she savored him, breathing him in, finding the seam that split the underside of his glans, her fingers ringing around him just beneath. She teased him with the tip of her tongue, curled it and cradled him.

He reached for her hair, tugged, biting off words that were gritty and raw, sex words, nasty words. She felt her sex swell and open, her juices ready to ease the way. She wanted him now and forever, filling her, beside her, with her.

Holding her mouth just so, she took him to the back of her throat, pressing her lips tight to his shaft as she pulled her way back to his cock's head. She stayed there, circling her cupped hand and her tongue over and around until she felt his balls tighten, his thighs and ass clench.

It would be so easy to give this to him, to let him finish, to come in her mouth, a pleasure they had shared last night, but she didn't. She let him go, crawling over his body, dragging her breasts, her belly, then her sex the length of his engorged cock.

"You're a cruel woman, Jamie Danby," he told her as she nuzzled his throat, his right armpit, his closest nipple that was as hard as hers. She flicked her tongue over it, massaged the muscle around it, the tips of her breasts skating through his chest hair as she moved from side to side. "Know I'll be getting back at you for this."

"I hope so," she said as she reached for a condom from those remaining on her nightstand. Throwing off the sheet, she sat on her knees and rolled the protective sheath to the base of his shaft. "If you don't, I'll have to hunt you down like a rabid dog."

He laughed, a guttural blast of sound, and grabbed both cheeks of her ass, urging her to take him, no, demanding that she did until she lowered her hips. Softly, she sat, impaled. Then she began to move, bracing her hands on his knees behind her, grinding, rotating, using her hips and her pelvis to dance, her clit sliding through the springy hair surrounding his thickness.

Sensation consumed her, sent her flying. Kell bucked his knees and she fell, planting her palms on either side of his pillowed head. He cupped her breasts, pushed them together, bit and kissed and licked his way from one peak to the other while she pumped up and down.

And then his eyes caught hers, held hers, refused to let her look away. All the things she saw… It was too much, the hope and the longing and the wishing and the want. How was she supposed to survive without him in her life? How was she supposed to pull out this memory years down the road and be happy when he wasn't with her?

Because she had no answer, she came, completely, giving herself up to the physical bliss of their joining. It was the most glorious pain, a beautiful ache.

She had him, but she didn't, and when he growled out, "Hands and knees," she gladly did his bidding, crawling off of him and onto the bed, punching a pillow beneath and anchoring her arms around it.

He knelt behind her, dug his fingers into her hips to position himself, then slid his palm over her sex, cupping her, slipping a thumb inside of her. His cock nudged his hand away, and he pushed into her slowly, releasing a groan that rattled her as his cock filled her up. He slid deeper, deeper, withdrew and returned, then reached around to toy with her clit, seeing to her pleasure while finding his own.

His strokes grew swifter, his breathing shallow; when he pulled his hand away to hold her hips, she replaced it with her own, working herself to completion as he came. He shuddered, stiffened, cursed coarsely and called her name. It made her cry, that sound, those words, though she buried her sobs in the pillow, hiding them.

Seconds later, the muscles of his thighs relaxed, and he moved away, easing himself from her body, then wrapping an arm around her waist and lowering them both to spoon.

They calmed together, no other words spoken, and then they showered, cleaning each other, Kell rinsing her, toweling her off, dressing while she dried her hair, fixing breakfast while she donned her weekend wardrobe of a tank top and shorts, and when time could no longer be forgotten, kissing her goodbye in her driveway.

It was a kiss full of tenderness, beauty, and she pressed her fingers to her lips to hold it there when he put his SUV into gear and backed into her street. He lingered, shaking his head as he settled his sunglasses in place. And when he finally pulled away, he burned strips of rubber into the pavement in front of her house.

A long black reminder of what she'd had and lost, one she'd see every day when she left for work and when she came home.

She returned to the cottage and spent the rest of the day—Saturday and Sunday, too—doing next to nothing but missing him. She didn't call her mother to tell her she was home. She did little more than move from the bed to the bathroom to the refrigerator, opening the door and staring inside.

When Monday morning arrived, she gathered her things, then exited through her half-acre backyard, opening the gate that led into Mr. Floyd's equally large yard behind and walking down Paul Revere Street instead of Lamplighter Lane.

Mr. Floyd wouldn't mind if she used his property as a shortcut in order to avoid the mark Kell had left in front of hers. It was either that, or never leave her cottage again.

As THEY'D PROMISED, Roni and Honoria had indeed taken care of things while Jamie'd been gone. That didn't mean she'd returned to find nothing to do. On the contrary. Her coworkers taking care of things simply meant they'd handled the daily chores that usually fell under her purview. It didn't mean they'd done her work, and she was glad.

Keeping busy meant she didn't have time to dwell on Kell's leaving her, or answer any questions Roni or Honoria had about what had happened while she was away. She didn't want to think about Midland. She didn't want to think about Kell or the hypnosis.

She didn't even want to think about what was going

on today—or had over the weekend—with the investigation into the Sonora Nites Diner murders. She wanted to think about the unpaid insurance claims and their deadlines staring her in the face. That was all.

She'd finally gone over everything about the trip and the hypnosis with her mother when Kate had stopped by the pediatrics clinic on her way to work. At least everything but the sex. Though Kell had called Jamie's mother while Captain Greenley had been conducting the exit interview following the session, Kate had wanted to hear the details firsthand.

As much as Jamie wanted to leave the last few days behind, she couldn't blame her mother for her curiosity or her concern. And though Jamie was certain her mother knew things with Kell had gone as they had, Kate didn't say a word. She just handed Jamie her coffee refill and told her they'd have dinner at Buck's Burger Barn tonight.

A burger sounded great, Jamie had to admit, heading to the lobby to cover the phones while Roni went on break. A burger wasn't a steak. A burger wasn't a bacon sandwich with Cheetos and tomato soup. A burger wouldn't make her think of Kell standing at her stove frying fresh-cut potatoes.

In fact, she was hungry enough that she didn't know how she was going to make it the two more hours until the clinic closed and she could get dinner, return to her sleepathon and start picking out names for her future cats. Gah, she had to stop. She was getting on her own nerves now.

When the front door opened, she welcomed the distraction from her depressing thoughts, smiling at the Hispanic man who approached. "May I help you?"

A shock of black hair falling over his forehead, he looked around, leaning his forearms on the reception counter, then finally gave Jamie his attention. "This office. It's the only kid doctor in Weldon? Me and my son, we just moved here."

Jamie nodded. "We are, yes. There's a general practitioner here as well, but you'll have to go to Alpine or Fort Stockton for another pediatrician. Were you wanting to make an appointment for your son?"

"School's coming up. He's going to need shots and things," he said, frowning, distracted, his dark eyes flitting but never to hers.

Jamie wondered if he was on drugs. "Sure. Do you have records from his last doctor? So we can see what he's had and what he needs?" she asked, opening the appointment-scheduling program and pulling the keyboard in front of her, prepared to input his information.

"His mother did all that. In Midland. I'll have to check."

"Did you want to go ahead and make the appointment? With school starting soon, we don't have a lot of openings in our schedule."

He shook his head, reached up to push back the fall of hair. "I'll just wait."

O…kay. She grabbed one of the clinic's cards and handed it across the counter. "Here's our number. Just give us a call when you're ready to come in."

He nodded, took it with a shaking hand, making Jamie think again of drugs. Or at least she thought of drugs until the cuff of his sleeve slipped up as he reached for the card and she saw his tattoo. The tattoo. The snake. Then she couldn't think of anything but not giving herself away.

For one short second, she considered asking for his name for their records, then thought better. She wouldn't do that with any other parent who wasn't ready to bring his child to see Dr. Griñon. This man might know that. This man might have been in here previously, before the hypnosis, and know that. And so she smiled and waited for him to go.

He studied the card, tapped it on the counter, then finally pushed away and headed for the door. Once he'd left the building, Jamie counted to thirty. She didn't want to jump up while he was right outside. She didn't want to start digging through the desk drawers for a letter opener or knife. She didn't want to pick up the phone and call for help until he couldn't walk back in and catch her.

Just as Jamie hit twenty-nine, Roni returned from her break. The other woman hadn't taken but one step into the lobby when Jamie whispered, "Lock the front door. Now. Turn the sign to Closed. And shut the blinds."

Roni frowned, but hurriedly did as she was told. Jamie picked up the phone, searching the desk for a weapon while she waited for Kell to pick up.

It took four rings before he did, and she could hear laughter in the background. His own voice sounded buoyant, upbeat. "Jamie?"

"He was here," she cried out with before he could say another word. "Here. In the office. I saw his tattoo."

"What? When? Maybe it was similar or—"

"Kell, it was it. The same one. I remember."

"Shit. Are you there alone?"

"No. Roni just locked the front door, and I'm holding a letter opener."

"Was he driving? Walking?" he asked, and Jamie could hear him shuffling his phone, slamming drawers.

She shoved out of Roni's chair and rushed to the door, flattening herself against the wall beside it to peer through the slats of the blinds. "There's a car pulling out of the lot. The glare's bad and the angle's wrong. I can't see if he's behind the wheel, but it's the only one."

"Can you get the tag numbers?"

Jamie gestured toward Roni who'd been standing and listening to her side of the conversation wide eyed. "Roni, help! Can you read the plates on that car?"

They talked over each other, Jamie seeing an eight where Roni saw a six, a three where she saw a five. It didn't matter. She rushed back to the desk, leaned across the counter, scrambled for a pen and wrote all of them down on her hand.

Then she read them to Kell. "I'm sorry. He was pulling away. That's the best we could do."

"You did good, sweetheart. We'll see what a mix and match turns up. Hang on a sec—" More shuffling sounds, cabinets banging, footsteps pounding, keys jangling, muffled voices in the background, until Kell came back. "You still there?"

"I'm here." She leaned her elbows on the counter, one hand holding the cordless phone, the other rubbing the bands of stress squeezing her forehead. She felt like a tomato ready to pop in a spray of red flesh and seeds.

"Okay. Troopers are on the way. No more than fifteen minutes. You stay in lockdown until they get there. Make sure all doors are secured. No one comes in or goes out."

She turned around, met the worried gazes of Roni and Honoria, who'd joined them, knew Mrs. Hernandez and her four-year-old-son would be right behind. "We've got patients here—"

"They can wait. No one, Jamie, you hear me? That door opens for no one unless they have a gun and a badge."

15

ON HIS RETURN TRIP to Weldon, Kell broke all land-speed records and abandoned every bit of common sense while behind the wheel. He'd been in his office at the ranger station when he took Jamie's call. His heart had yet to return to its normal rhythm. After the shock it had taken, he was surprised it was beating at all.

He'd kept her on the line until the first two troopers had arrived at Weldon Pediatrics. It had been a hell of an agonizing wait, working to keep his calm while insisting she do the same. A wait made worse by his being torn between doing the right thing as a ranger, and doing the right thing as a man whose woman's life was at risk.

He knew there was a DPS unit that regularly patrolled Texas 17 between Weldon and Balmorhea. Knew, too, they were his best hope for tracking down the suspect. If the Sonora Nites Diner killer was in the car Jamie had seen, he hadn't had time to get far.

It had been a gut-wrenching decision to make, but Kell had given those officers Jamie's description of the two-door sedan, the possible combinations of tag numbers, the location and look of the driver's tattoo. The unit that worked the stretch of highway between Weldon and Alpine was the one he'd sent to see to Jamie at work.

He'd been three hours out when she'd called. Three hours he'd cut to almost two by running with his grille lights flashing. He'd waited until hearing that the troopers were at the clinic before he'd let Jamie go and called Dr. Kate.

When he pulled up in front of Weldon Pediatrics, a sheen of sweat dampening his skin, his heart still pumping high-octane fuel, he found Jamie's mother waiting for him in her Suburban just like he'd asked. He pulled his SUV alongside hers and got out, staying her from doing the same with the wave of his hand.

She rolled down her window instead, and beneath the brim of the ball cap she'd pulled low to shield her eyes from the sun, her frown furrowed with fury. "What the hell is going on with my daughter?"

He'd told Jamie not to call her mother, or let the others in the office call family members or friends until the troopers assessed the situation. He wanted to avoid a flood of concerned loved ones descending and raising a battle cry.

This wasn't the scene of a crime. It was unlikely there was evidence to disturb outside; gravel dust didn't hold tire tracks. Fingerprints, shoe prints, strands of hair left inside were a different matter. But keeping a lid on things until he knew what they were facing would keep speculation from blowing like seeds on the wind.

"She's fine. Did you pack her things and enough food for a week?" Kell asked, thumbing his hat up his forehead. Whatever the investigation brought to light, he was not leaving Jamie here. And he was not bringing her back until the bastard was behind bars.

"I did, but I'm not handing them over until I get an answer," Kate said, her hand gripping the strap of the duffel bag in her passenger seat. Two boxes and an extra-large cooler took up most of the back. "When you called me from Midland? Right after the hypnosis session? You told me she didn't remember anything you could use."

Kell wanted to get to Jamie, but her mother deserved consideration. She was the one who'd brought Jamie safely this far. He propped a forearm on the roof of the Suburban, staring into the distance at the Davis Mountains rolling like waves in the haze.

"I told you she remembered the tattoo on the killer's wrist."

"Right. And?"

"And, she just saw it again."

"What? Where? Here?" Kate looked around frantically. "I want to see her. Now."

He held the door handle, preventing her from climbing down from her seat. "Wait. Hear me out. The man is gone. Jamie is fine. She and her coworkers are inside, and the troopers have secured the building. We can't let anyone else go in until we get the place dusted for prints, and see what other trace evidence he might've left behind."

Kate didn't like hearing what he had to say, but she didn't fight him for the door. "But you're bringing her out?"

He nodded. "And then I'm taking her someplace

safe. I know she'll argue, so having you on my side would go a long way to helping convince her."

With a huff, Kate sat back, crossed her arms over her leopard-print scrubs and glared. "I'm not so sure she'll be safe with you. He found her just days after you brought her home? Hardly a coincidence. I'd say your office needs to be checked for leaks. And I don't mean just some careless talk," she added, her tone brutally condemning. "What if someone there has known the killer's identity all these years? And not turned him in for that horrific crime? What kind of person could do something that unconscionable?"

Kell had imagined the same worst-case scenario seconds into Jamie's call, and had asked himself the same questions, though he was still weighing the possibilities. "He could've been here all this time, keeping an eye on her to see if her memory returned."

He could tell from the shake of her head that Kate wasn't buying it. "Or the story in the paper last week could have brought him here." Though this conversation was one he should be having with the authorities on the scene instead of with Kate, sounding it out with Jamie's mother couldn't hurt as a first step.

"Yeah, he could've come because of the article, to see if his face rang any bells," Kell said again. "But if he knew about the hypnosis… That was when Jamie remembered that he was Hispanic and tattooed. Either he knew that and wanted to see her reaction to his ink, or he didn't know, and was looking for any reaction, any refreshed memories at all."

"Six of one, half dozen of the other," Kate said with

a dismissive wave of her hand. "He came here to find out if she could ID him."

"And assuming she didn't give anything away—"

"I hope you're not basing your investigation on assumptions," she interrupted him to say. "We've assumed all this time she was safe here. We've assumed he had no plans to risk exposure by coming after her. I'm done with assumptions."

"No, ma'am. No assumptions. From here on, we work with solid evidence and facts."

"Sergeant Harding!"

Kell took a step in reverse and glanced over the hood of his SUV toward the officer flagging him down from outside the clinic's door. He waved that he was on his way, then told Jamie's mother, "I'll bring her out. Can you throw her pack and the supplies in the backseat with my things?"

Kate opened her door, turning on her seat to face him. "Only if you promise me you'll bring her home in one piece, and only when it's safe."

"Yes, ma'am. I promise." He slapped the hood of his vehicle then jogged toward the clinic. Enough of a crowd had gathered that two of the officers were positioning their cruisers to form a barricade.

He wanted to get Jamie out of here, but he first had to speak to the officers on scene and the civilians still inside. Doing so would go down a lot easier without any distractions—which meant sending her with a trooper to wait with Kate. He pulled Deputy Aronson aside and asked him to take care of that while Kell did what he needed to do.

Though it took an hour to finish his questioning, Kell learned nothing from Jamie's female coworkers, or from the doctor, or from the patients who'd been in the clinic when the man with the snake tattooed on his wrist had come in. Jamie had been the only one to see him.

Kell was interrupted twice during his interviews, hearing first from the troopers who'd gone after the car. No luck yet with them, or with the technician at the ranger station running the tag numbers on her end. Hitting dead end after dead end did not sit well with Kell.

This case had gone unsolved too long already. He'd be damned if he let this first solid lead they'd had in years go cold. Once he finished his initial investigation and made sure the officers knew he'd be in touch, he headed for his SUV, Jamie and Kate.

The two women were standing between the two vehicles, heads together, Kate's arm around her daughter's shoulders, Jamie holding on to her mother's free hand. Aviator sunglasses covering his eyes, Deputy Aronson stood next to the rear of Kell's SUV, arms crossed, stance wide, blocking the only entrance to the triangle of space where the Danby family stood.

That was what got to Kell. Jamie and Dr. Kate were the entire family, a fictional family created to save Jamie's life. They were two alone, depending solely on one another. Kell had his parents, his brothers, plus aunts and uncles and cousins he saw only a couple of times a year but knew he could tap in an emergency. He also had the Texas Department of Public Safety at his back, coworkers in numbers dwarfing what the Danby women had, and his carried weapons.

The injustice of their situation rankled. Seeing them as victims left him vexed. Yes, their circumstances were only unique to them; he'd dealt with dozens, hundreds of human casualties as he fought the war against crime, each with their own story, their own nightmares, but from those he'd kept his distance. Why he hadn't kept it this time…

Oh, hell. Who was he kidding? He knew exactly why he hadn't kept it this time. He'd walked through the front door of Weldon Pediatrics and seen that ponytail swinging, those big eyes dancing, those freckles spattering that nose, and that ass. She'd done him in, right then, right there; the teddy-bear scrubs hadn't helped.

And then he'd seen the fear, the devastating realization that her life was coming undone, that her carefully constructed wall of Jericho was tumbling down around her. He was a lawman, a savior, a rescuer. The fact that she was a damsel in distress in name only didn't keep him from wanting to be a full-fledged, bona fide white knight.

Once he'd released Deputy Aronson from guard duty, Kell approached the two women who, ready or not, were now going to have to say their goodbyes. As he passed, he glanced through his open driver's-side window into the SUV's backseat. Good. Jamie's pack was there with the cooler and boxes.

She looked up at his approach. Her face was pale, her eyes red-rimmed but dry. He needed to question her in detail, but they had a long drive waiting and plenty of time. For now, all he asked her was, "Ready?"

Her nod was brief. She knew nothing of where they were going. All he'd told her while they'd been on the phone was that he was coming to take her away.

"Give me a minute?" she asked.

"A minute," he said, concern a whetstone making his voice sharp, then walked around to the passenger door. He opened it. He waited. Through the window on the other side, he watched as she hugged Dr. Kate. As gripped as his gut was, he couldn't imagine what the Danby women were feeling, and when one minute became two, he still didn't move.

Minute three ticked around, and now his impatience caused him to clear his throat. Jamie stepped back, letting her mother's hand linger in her own until the distance grew and Kate's fingers slipped away. She climbed into her seat without saying a word to Kell.

He stayed where he was, waiting, and when she met his gaze, it was all he could do to nod toward her seat belt and tell her, "Buckle up."

The emotion in her face socked him in the solar plexus as hard as any hit he'd ever taken. Fists, football helmets, baseball bats. Brennan wailing on him after Kell had gone out with Lauren Randall, Brennan's crush. Terry wiping out his skateboard in front of Kell's and sending them both to the pavement where they'd broken bones. None of those incidents had left him feeling as hammered as the feelings Jamie couldn't hold back, a mixture of anger and fear and loathing.

He closed her door, made his way around to his and stopped to offer Kate his hand. She shook it, said nothing as she released it, just climbed behind the wheel of her Suburban and sprayed rooster tails of gravel as she drove away.

Kell remained silent as well, putting on his seat belt,

adjusting his visor, settling his hat so low that it bumped his sunglasses' frames. The sun would be hanging on the horizon a couple more hours, but the day was still bright, hot, dry. Outside, anyway. Inside the SUV, he swore he could safely store a side of beef.

He understood Jamie not being happy with the state of things. Working this case wasn't remotely how he'd hoped he'd be spending his time. They were both going to have to deal, and cross their fingers that they'd come out in one piece on the other side.

Once Weldon was behind them, he breathed deeply and nudged up the brim of his hat. "I know you told me everything on the phone, but I want you to tell me again."

"Why? Nothing's going to change," she said, her gaze fixed out her window, one hand gripping the edge of her seat, the other doing the same damage to her armrest. "I remember it all. I don't need to give you a mind's-eye narrative to have my memory refreshed."

Part of him wanted to growl. Another part wanted to laugh. He grabbed for middle ground. "I need the narrative. I know you told me everything, but I had a lot of things on my mind when you did. Mainly, securing your safety. I might've missed a detail that could've sparked a question with an answer that would help."

She seemed to give that consideration because she released her hold on the SUV's interior and sank into the seat. "It was a little bit after three. Roni goes on break then and I cover the front desk. I'd been on the phone with a sales rep wanting to schedule time with Dr. Griñon, and was late relieving her. Five or ten minutes."

Good. An established timeline.

"She headed to the break room—"

"Were there any patients in the lobby then?"

"No. The Irigoyen twins were due at three-thirty for their six-month checkup. Emilio Duran should've been there, but rescheduled his school sports physical." Jamie's voice softened. "Dr. Griñon has been his pediatrician since birth. I think the other guys on the team give him a hard time about a baby doctor clearing him for football."

Kell was intimately familiar with high-school locker-room razzing. "So you were there by yourself when this guy came in. And he didn't set off any bells? Fidgeting, looking around, avoiding eye contact? Asking questions but not really paying attention?"

"He looked around, yes, but as far as I knew, he'd never been in the clinic, so I didn't think anything of it. He was rather…twitchy, though. I wondered if he might be on drugs, yes. It wasn't the normal inquisitiveness of a father dealing with child custody for the first time, immunizations for school, stuff like that. It was more like…he didn't want to be there."

"Why did you think he was dealing with child custody?"

"When I asked if he had his son's medical records, he said his wife had taken care of all of that in Midland."

Midland. Kell wondered if the man had pulled that location out of thin air, or if he had a connection to the city Kell called home. The city where Company E was headquartered. And in light of his earlier conversation with Jamie's mother, the speculation about a leak in the department…

His gut souring as it churned, he checked his rearview and side mirrors before prodding Jamie for more. "Tell me about seeing the tattoo."

She took her time responding, staring out the window at the endless acres of yellowed grazing land, acres too dry to sustain more than the few head of cattle dotting them. "I saw it when I handed him a card with the clinic's phone number and office hours. He didn't want to make an appointment then, or have me open a file for his son. So I told him if he wanted to have him seen before school started, to call soon. Our schedule's always full this time of year. He was wearing long sleeves, and the cuff slid up when he took the card."

Long sleeves. In August. Laborers wore them, in the oil fields, on farms and ranches. Construction and road crews even. "Did he look like he'd been working? Or smell like it? Sweaty, dusty, anything?"

"Not that I noticed." She paused, added, "Oh, but his hair was clean. It kept falling over his forehead. Why do you ask?"

"The long sleeves. Whether he's our guy or not, he could be working in the area."

"An illegal?"

He grimaced, nodded. "Yeah, most likely. And if he smelled like plywood or diesel fuel or fertilizer or road tar, it would give us an idea of where he might be employed, who to question that might be able to identify him…"

"You don't think he was on his way to work, do you?"

"I doubt it," Kell said, shaking his head. "Were the cuffs buttoned? Loose?"

"I don't know," she snapped. "Why does it matter?"

Her exasperation only made the conclusions he was drawing that much harder to face. But he wasn't going to deceive her, or hide what he was thinking. After all she'd done to help his investigation, she deserved his honesty.

"I'm trying to determine what he wanted from you. Hear me out," he added when she turned to interrupt. "If he's been here all this time, he likely heard about Kass Duren's body being ID'd, and he could've been feeling you out, seeing if you would recognize his face, or his voice. Showing you the tattoo when his cuff slipped up could've been nothing.

"But," Kell continued, trying to corral his thinking into words, "if he knew you'd been through the forensic hypnosis, and knew you'd remembered the tattoo, he very well could've been gauging your reaction to seeing it again, and the fact that you didn't react—"

"Is the only reason I'm alive," she said, catching up to his train of thought. "The first scenario would mean he's been around all these years, watching me. And the second…"

Angry enough to spit mortars, Kell finished the sentence for her. "The second means there's a leak in the department, and I dragged you from your safe existence out into the open."

16

JAMIE WOKE TO COMPLETE darkness. Not the darkness she was used to in her bedroom at night, but a darkness so thick, she saw nothing. She knew she was in Kell's SUV, and wherever they'd stopped, they hadn't been here long; the interior was still warm, though missing him.

It had been almost seven before they'd left Weldon. Since Kell hadn't wanted to stop until they reached their destination, he'd asked one of the troopers to pick them up burgers and fries from Juan Cantu's. From the clinic, they'd headed south; from a distance, a cruiser had followed.

Traveling back roads she hadn't known existed, Kell had stopped only once—in a town smaller than Weldon for gas. He'd told her the maneuvers were to guarantee no one but the troopers stuck to their tail, and the troopers were to dissuade anyone stupid enough to try tailing them. If the man with the tattoo was indeed their murder suspect, he'd have no bread crumbs to track to find them.

She needed to use the bathroom. She need to stretch her legs, her back and arms. She was used to moving all day, not sitting, not riding. She needed something besides the melted ice from their to-go order to drink.

But Kell was calling the shots, so she waited. His endless stream of questions before she'd told him she was spent, dried up, out of words, had made her situation perfectly clear. One wrong move—intentional or accidental—could undo all his precautions.

She was aggravated, inconvenienced, irritated, afraid. But she was not stupid. And so she pulled her knees to her chest and curled in on herself, waiting.

Moments later, she heard what sounded like footsteps on planking, and raised her forehead from the cradle of her knees in time to see Kell descending a set of porch steps in front of a small log structure.

Warm yellow light spilled from the doorway, illuminating his way to the front of his SUV. And then she remembered that he'd told her about this place. He fished here, hunted, holed up to get away.

Jamie lowered her feet to the floor and sat forward, waiting as he came around to open her door to the smells of earth and pine and midnight, as he moved into the bright wedge of space there and smiled.

"Sleep well?" he asked.

She nodded. She guessed she had. She'd drifted off before the sun had set, and hadn't even stirred when he'd parked. "What time is it?"

"Ten-thirty or so." He gestured toward the cabin. "I fed the generator and turned on the water. I need to haul in the food from the cooler, but that can wait. I'd rather you get settled first."

She'd been out of sorts earlier, resenting him. Now she could only remember how thoughtful he was, how strong and kind, how cute. She climbed from her seat and stepped into his arms. He groaned and wrapped her up tight.

"Does that mean you forgive me?"

"There's nothing to forgive."

"I know none of this is easy," he said, using the heel of his palm to massage the length of her spine.

She shivered, snuggling even closer. Being in his arms felt so good, so right. "I'm pretty sure life's not supposed to be. At least not all of it."

"Maybe not. But this goes above and beyond what most people face."

"In case you haven't noticed yet, I'm not most people."

He leaned back far enough to see her expression, and stared at her for a long moment, seeming to weigh which thoughts were safe to share, and which were best kept private as he brushed strands of hair away from her eyes.

She wondered about his private thoughts, if they mirrored hers in considering the possibility that they'd been thrown together by fate—and for more personal reasons than solving the Sonora Nites Diner murders.

But he gave nothing away when he said, "I've noticed a lot of things about you. Some of them you may not like."

Uh-oh? "Such as?"

"You snore."

She huffed. "What? I do not."

"You do. And I've got the broken right eardrum to prove it."

He was teasing her, she knew it, trying to keep things light. She appreciated the effort, deciding two could play this game. She pulled away, punched his shoulder, too emotionally spent to be embarrassed over what was more than likely the truth. "I'm sure that was just the hum of all that equipment running there on your dash."

"Trust me. It wasn't a hum."

Okay. Now he was asking for it, she mused, fighting a grin. She could dish back to him as much teasing snark as he delivered. She stomped around him, heading for the porch steps, and calling over her shoulder. "I hope you've got an extra bed because I'll be sleeping alone in yours."

Behind her, he whooped and hollered and cackled like a hyena, and she decided then and there that she loved him.

THEY SLEPT TOGETHER. They didn't have sex. Kell spooned behind her, an arm securing her, and kept her close to his body most of the night. When they'd last been in bed together, he'd told her he wasn't a cuddler and not to take it personally. Now she was left trying to figure out how to interpret that he didn't want to let her go.

With so much on her mind, she woke before he did, and though she lay there soaking him up as long as she could, eventually nature called. As quietly as possible, she slid from the bed. While in the telephone booth of a bathroom, she washed her hands and face, then tiptoed barefoot to the front of the cabin.

Kell had left her backpack on the sofa with his, and brought in the food her mother had gathered at his request. He'd done all that, however, after tucking Jamie into bed wearing her undies. It had been too dark—and too late—to do any looking around, so she found her sandals, a pair of khaki knee shorts, a white camisole tank top, and then she found the back door.

Kell's cabin sat in a valley; she assumed in the Guadalupe Mountains since they'd left the Davis range behind. He'd taken a long and winding circuitous route, and when the sun had set, it had made off with her sense of direction.

From the back porch, she could see the sun teasing the tops of the rocky peaks, and she guessed it was between eight and ten. Either way, she was surprised Kell wasn't up and on the phone. She was also surprised at the sense of absolute peace that enveloped her as she braced a shoulder on a rough-hewn beam and leaned, arms crossed, into the railing.

The day would be miserably hot before it was over, but for now, she welcomed the dry warmth, the air that smelled of piñon and raw earth. She didn't pick up wafts of spicy meats cooking, the way she did when walking to and from work and passed the Cantus'. She didn't catch the scents of exhaust and farm animals that were constants in Weldon. She smelled solitude and comfort and calm.

She breathed deeply, realizing, when she finally heard Kell stirring inside, that her blood was stirring, too, in anticipation. And then she smelled coffee and smiled. Life. The only way it could get any better would be for her not to be in danger of losing hers. She didn't want to lose it. Especially not when she'd just found her place and her man.

Oh, that sounded so good. Her man. She knew she was running on adrenaline, endorphins, and those hormones had a lot to do with her state of mind. The state of her heart was another thing. She hadn't stopped thinking about Kell since meeting him.

Yes, he was working her case and that had brought them into contact. But her thoughts weren't about bloodshed and loss. She thought about the way his eyes crinkled at the corners, the way his mouth did the same when he smiled. She thought about his teeth and his tongue, the pressure of his lips against hers.

She thought about his brothers. Brennan. Terry, whose full name was Terrance, he'd told her. She thought about his mother decorating his house, about his father teaching Kell how to cobble together a computer to cut costs—all stories Kell had shared over their reheated soup and sandwiches before they'd returned from Midland to Weldon.

She thought about his mentor, a family friend, being the lead investigator on the murder case, how Kell was now honoring Warren Sheets by continuing his work. He was an honorable man, her Kell. A good man she was going to fight for. Now that she'd had a taste of the real thing, she couldn't see herself settling comfortably into spinsterhood, even with a daily cup of tea with JB, and a calico cat for company.

Behind her, the door onto the railed and covered porch opened, and Kell came out, two cups of coffee in hand. He had on jeans. Worn jeans. Tight jeans. The lower legs bunched at the tops of his boots. His gray athletic T-shirt hung loose. She didn't know if she was happier to see him or the coffee.

"Good morning. Did I wake you?"

He nodded as he sipped.

"I didn't mean to."

"It's quiet out here. I'm going to wake to any noise.

Especially when I realize that it's you making it." He sipped again. "I like you here with me."

"Because you know I'm safe?"

"That, but mostly because I like you."

She felt her heart beating harder, and she turned away to look at the view. Hope was hard for her. She didn't know what to do with it, how to respond without giving too much of herself away. He might like her, but he might not be ready for the things she was feeling.

And really—she needed to find out first how ready she was herself. "How often do you spend time out here?"

"You like it?"

"What's not to like? I can smell more than vomit and antiseptic. I can hear more than crying babies and excuses from insurance companies for not paying claims."

"I thought you enjoyed your job."

She nodded, cradled her cup in both hands and lifted it to her mouth. "I do. But this is the first time in all the years I've worked there that I've taken a break."

Kell moved to stand beside her, leaning a hip against the porch railing. "You're either extremely dedicated or insane. All work and no play makes Jamie a—"

"A woman who's figured out that staying busy is the best way to live in the moment," she said. "Instead of…"

"Instead of dwelling on the past," he finished for her.

Bringing her history to this idyllic place had not been her intent, but the words had slipped out before she could stop them. "Yes. And I'm sorry for bringing it up."

"We're here because of your past. We're together because of your past."

Were they together? Or were they both just here? She

glanced at him, found him studying her intently, his eyes gravely serious over the rim of his cup. She wanted to look away. She didn't want him to see the things she was thinking. She didn't want to let slip words he wasn't ready to hear.

And so she started to turn, to focus on her coffee and the scrub brush and stunted trees struggling to stay alive beyond Kell's clearing. He reached for her drink, took it from her hand, set her cup and his on the table between the two porch rockers behind them. Then he reached for her.

He moved her to face him, his hands on her waist, and lifted her to sit on the railing. She draped her wrists over his shoulders, hooked her heels around his thighs and held on as he came to stand between her spread legs.

His expression was that of a lover, compassionate, involved, present. His words ones she needed desperately to hear. "I can deal with your past, Jamie. It's not going to scare me away."

Did he know she'd thought that it might? "You're a Texas Ranger, Kell. I think not running away from a crime is part of your job description."

He shook his head. "That's not what I'm talking about. And I'm pretty sure you know it."

She did. That was the thing that scared her. "I'm trying not to read anything into anything. I'd rather rely on what I know is real."

"Then let me show you what's real," he said, and lowered his mouth to hers.

He tasted like coffee. Sugar and cream and beans grown on an Indonesian hillside. And he tasted like

Kell, smelled like Kell. She'd come to know his scent and his taste. He was so familiar already. She knew his movements, too, the insistent thrust of his tongue juxtaposed with the tentative request for entry.

She brought him closer with her heels, her hands, her longing. Beneath the cotton of her camisole, her breasts tightened. Beneath her khaki shorts, her sex grew damp. His kiss did this to her. Made her body ache, weep, want. And kissing him back nearly broke her heart. How would she ever in her lifetime get enough of him?

Needing space, time…sanity, she pulled away, dropped her head onto her shoulders and closed her eyes. Kell was quiet; she knew he was watching her, knew he could see the buttons of her nipples pressing into the fabric of her top. She wanted him to see, wanted him to know. Wanted him to want her, to crave the way she did.

Holding her waist with one hand, he skated his knuckles over her breasts, the peaks, the swells, one side then the other. When she grew dizzy, wobbling, her head spinning, her equilibrium lost in lust, he helped her ease down from the railing. But he was too late.

She'd already fallen for him hard. That's why she wondered if she wasn't hearing things when he told her, "Let's get out of our clothes…and go for a swim."

17

THE WATER in the spring-fed pond on Kell's property measured close to seventy-five degrees Fahrenheit year-round, making it possible to go for a cooling swim in the summer, or a dip to warm up during the months when the air and the ground were freezing outside.

Kell had never been in it with a girl. He'd been here with his brothers, with fellow lawmen. Those swims tended to involve a lot of barbecue, beer and betting on the Super-Bowl or the Final Four. He'd never cannonballed into the center and surfaced, sputtering, to find a woman wearing her underwear waiting on the end of the dock.

Especially one who knew how to swim, but didn't like to, who preferred to dangle her feet in the water from above, to watch it lap at the shoreline. Silly woman. At least he'd finally managed to get her to agree to join him.

"Just so we're clear," Jamie said sternly, her hands on her hips as she stared down, grimacing. "We are not having sex in the water. I don't care how clean you say it is."

Until she'd said it, he hadn't even thought about sex… Okay, he'd sorta thought it, but not seriously… Okay, he'd been serious, but pretty sure she'd say no. Which she had. "Just jump."

"I'm not going to break my neck, am I?"

"Not if you jump in feetfirst. Don't dive. Just jump."

"You're sure I won't die?"

"Only if I come up there and strangle you." The woman was nuts. She killed him, and he didn't know how he'd ever get enough. "Now jump!"

She turned around, took several retreating steps, enough to make him nervous that she might actually leave, then stopped, spun and ran, launching off the end of the dock in a flying leap, screaming, then grabbing her nose to pinch it closed before going under the water.

A huge grin on his face, Kell waited for her to come up. She did nearly immediately, shaking her head, her hair flying, water drops splattering all around her. He swam toward her, chuckling, taking on mouthfuls of water he spit out when he stopped.

"Nice jump," he told her, his legs and arms stroking the water, his face aching from his grin.

"Nice water," she told him, moving similarly, though without the same joyful expression. And then she scrunched up her eyes. "Wait a minute. Are those fish I keep feeling?"

"They are. Mexican tetra. Pupfish. They're harmless." He didn't tell her about the tetras belonging to the piranha family.

Treading water, she looked at him, one dark wet brow arched. "I never thought you would be the one to send me to swim with the fishes."

Kell's laugh echoed around them—until Jamie brought her hand down on the water's surface in a splat that sent a huge splash into his face. He caught his breath, held it, flipped ass over end and dived into the clear pool.

He grabbed her feet and tugged her with him, releasing her before she had time to react, then surfacing right behind her. She turned, the wicked gleam in her eye his only warning. She kicked out and launched forward, her hands on his shoulders pushing him down.

They chased each other from one side of the pond to the other, tussling, attacking, choking when laughing and going under with open mouths. Kell couldn't remember the last time he'd played like a kid, or had this much fun with a woman without being in bed. He was pretty sure he never had, and what a crying shame.

Exhausted after an hour of horseplay fueled by coffee and camaraderie, they wordlessly agreed to a cease-fire, floating lazily to catch their breath before heading for the dock. Kell boosted Jamie up first, then followed. Dripping and spent, he collapsed on his back. She sat on the end, legs dangling.

Eyes scrunched against the sun, he eventually forced himself onto his elbows. They needed to get clothes on before Jamie especially got burned. His T-shirt was here somewhere… "Now are you going to tell me why you don't like swimming?"

She afforded him an over-the-shoulder look. "I almost drowned when I was six. I fell into the deep end of a private pool our church had rented for the summer. Parents dropped off their kids for the afternoon, picked them up before dinner."

He sat up the rest of the way. "That was a long time ago. And you are a very good swimmer."

She shrugged, and he wished he could see her face. "I guess all the years after, I only remembered the fright, not the fun."

Still… "But you did have fun. Today."

"No. I was faking. Like I always do." She glanced back again, winked, returned to facing away. Then, with Kell still looking for the humor in what she'd just said, she sighed with her entire body, braced her palms behind her and leaned back. "I think I could live here. I can't believe that you don't. That you live in suburbia instead."

"Hell of a long commute to Midland," was all he said, curious to see where she was taking this. He was still stuck on her faking it.

"Can you imagine raising a family here?"

This was where he came to unwind, to forget what he came up against the rest of the time. Living here would make it hard to do either. Then again, he'd never thought of living here with her. Or of raising a family… "A bit isolated, don't you think?"

"That's what makes it so perfect." She sat forward again, tucked her crossed legs beneath her, looked all around. "You'd have to clear more of the property. Add on to the cabin at some point. Put in a barn and corral for horses. Section off a spot for a vegetable garden."

The horses he could see. The larger cabin, too. He'd want dogs. Five at least. But a garden? "Have you ever tried to grow anything in what passes for soil out here?"

"Raised beds, then. A greenhouse, even. With a separate area for flowers. God, I could spend hours—" And just like that, she cut herself off, reaching up to press her palm to her forehead as if pushing her thoughts back inside.

Was she embarrassed to be caught dreaming? Or was it that she was dreaming about his place, and he assumed by extension, him? Was there more to her dream than a vegetable greenhouse and horses? He thought back to what she'd said…

Ah, a place to start looking for answers. He moved closer, sitting beside her on the end of the dock, his navy board shorts making puddles that spread toward her. "What about the isolation makes it perfect, Jamie?"

She stared down at the water where Kell could see the tiny tetra schooling. "The quiet. The privacy. Swimming in your underwear and not worrying about an audience."

He smiled at that. "I would think quiet and privacy were both abundant in Weldon."

"Not enough that I can swim in my underwear."

"You don't have a pool," he told her, knowing this wasn't about what she wore swimming at all. "What's going on, Jamie? Tell me what you're thinking."

She blew out a puff of breath, closed her eyes, shook her head. "It's so stupid—"

"It's not stupid."

"You haven't heard it yet."

"Only because you haven't said it. I'm waiting. I'm listening—"

"I'm thinking that if I'd lived someplace like this all these years, he wouldn't have found me."

He could tell by the way she'd blurted it that she was tired of holding it in as much as she was embarrassed by entertaining the thought. But they both knew if the suspect was determined, he would've found her even if she'd been hiding in the desert in Tunisia.

What he needed to do now was make her see that it was okay for her to be scared.

"The home you and your mother made in Weldon? Best thing you could have done. Warren worked his ass off looking for a way to circumvent the rules and regs of witness protection, but there was no pending trial, no suspect for you to testify against…"

Kell shook his head, remembering the mornings he'd come into the office to find that his mentor had never gone home. "Well, he tried. And he was glad to see you and Kate safely settled as the Danbys."

"He helped us a lot. With the red tape of changing our names. I know my mother asked his opinion on the places she was considering before she moved us." She paused a moment, picked a splinter of wood from the edge of the dock, tossed it into the pond. "Now I wonder why we bothered."

"You can't mean that."

"Sure I can. We were never safe. Not if he was living nearby and watching. Even if he wasn't, he had no trouble finding us—"

"He had help. If he knew about the hypnosis through a leak, then that same leak would have told him where to find you." Kell's phone calls this morning while the coffee had brewed were as much about locating the information's source as its destination.

"Like I said." She shrugged, got to her feet. "Never safe."

Kell waited several seconds, then stood, too. He didn't want to burst her bubble, but… "You wouldn't have been any safer here."

"I could have seen him coming."

Because of the wide-open spaces? Maybe if the clearing around the cabin and pond was expanded like she'd suggested he do. As it was, getting close to the cabin without being seen would not be that hard. The thought had Kell lifting his head, looking around. He'd taken every possible precaution on the trip—

Son of a bitch. Son of a bitch! He'd told no one but Norm Greenley where he and Jamie would be. That didn't mean it would take a rocket scientist to think to look here. He talked about his property often. His name was on the deed, and a search of tax records would give anyone looking the exact location.

Shit and double shit. If he'd been using the head on his shoulders instead of introducing Jamie to the one in his pants, he would've realized he could put an end to this thing today. All he had to do was get Greenley to let slip the location where he'd stashed Jamie.

Once the information was out in the open, the leak in the Midland office—assuming that's what had happened—would feed the details to the killer. When the bastard showed up, Kell and his army would be waiting.

He reached for her elbow, turned her toward him. "Hey, we need to get you out of the sun before you crisp. And as much fun as I'm having here, I need to check in with my team."

She pulled away, lifted her hand to shade her eyes. "Did you talk to them earlier?"

He nodded, and started walking in reverse, motioning for her to come with him. "While making coffee, yeah."

"And nothing?" she asked, following. "No sign of the car?"

"Not yet," he said. But all that was about to change.

18

ONCE BACK AT THE CABIN, Jamie left Kell to his laptop and phone—both connected to civilization through satellite links—and headed for the shower. It was the size of a stamp in the telephone-booth bathroom. She bumped her elbows on the enclosure's walls when raising her arms to scrub her hair. If Kell ever added onto the cabin, he'd have to do something about this space…

God, why was she even going there? She couldn't believe she'd talked to him as if they were a couple discussing remodeling plans. She'd even talked about raising a family here. She hadn't mentioned the two of them, but he had to know that's what she'd been thinking.

The worst part was, she didn't know why she'd been thinking about kids when she'd decided long ago having a family was not in her future. No, the worst part was that she did.

Kell would make the most wonderful father. She could see him roughhousing and romping and wrestling with sons and daughters, teaching them right from wrong, helping them with their reading, writing and 'rithmetic.

He was just that kind of guy. He made her think of

home and hearth, of family. Her childhood had been fairly all-American, her parents high-school sweethearts, doting and in love. When her father left, it hadn't been about his relationship with her mother falling apart.

No, he hadn't been strong enough to face what Jamie—Stephanie—had been through. He couldn't deal with what she'd seen, what she'd suffered. The one time in her life she'd needed him more than any other, and he'd walked, incapable of finding the internal strength to be her rock. Pathetic. She hadn't seen him since.

She couldn't imagine Kell doing that. Ever. It was there in everything he did. The responsibility he took. The concern he showed. The way he talked about his brothers with such fondness, about his parents with such respect. His intelligence, his sense of humor, she loved it all.

She loved him.

She sank to her haunches, burying her face in her hands. Water pelted her back, stinging. Yes, she'd known him but a handful of days. Tomorrow would be a week. He'd come to her rescue. But this wasn't that. She swore it wasn't that. She was not infatuated with the man who had saved her.

She was in love with the man who'd walked into the clinic, a gun at his hip and a glint in his eye. The man who was everything she wanted in a partner, one she'd thought her circumstances would deny her. Kell had laid her worries to rest, telling her he wasn't scared, he wasn't running away. And he'd said it as a man, not as a Texas Ranger.

It had to be enough for now. And it was, she thought, making herself leave the enclosure before he came looking to see if she'd dissolved down the drain. She was not going to push him, or pry to see what she could get him to divulge of his feelings. At least not until they were beyond this nightmare and could see the light of day.

Once dressed, she headed for the kitchen that was really just an alcove off the main room and part of the dining area. Kell sat at the table there, his jeans again caught up in the tops of his boots, though he now wore a chambray shirt, the sleeves rolled up his forearms, the khaki setting off the color the sun had left on his skin.

When he realized she had stopped to stare, he looked up. And he smiled, with his mouth, with his eyes, with what looked like his heart. "Ready to eat?"

She nodded, swallowed. Her voice had to be here somewhere. "I'll fix something. You've got work."

"There are staples in the cupboard, and the fresh stuff isn't fancy."

She pulled open the refrigerator door to see what her mother had packed them. Ground beef, sandwich meats, hot dogs, chicken breasts. There was bread and buns and condiments. "Burgers okay?"

"Sure. You want me to light a fire in the grill?" He scooted back his chair, but stayed put. "Or there's an iron skillet if you'd rather brown 'em on the stove."

She'd rather he not make her think about cooking for him for the rest of their lives. Not now. Not yet. "You work. I'll cook. It's the nature of things."

He laughed then, a gusty blast of sound that curled her toes. He'd brought this into her life, too. Laughter that was hale and hearty and male, and made her long to jump into his arms and hug him. Instead, she reached for one of the pounds of ground beef wrapped in butcher paper and tossed it onto the countertop. It landed with a thud.

"Anything new on the case?" she asked, squatting to find the iron skillet in the cabinet next to the stove. It was just dusty enough that she cleaned it before setting it on the gas burner to heat. And in the pantry beside the back door, she found a lazy Susan with spices—salt, pepper, garlic and chili powder for an extra kick.

She unrolled the package of meat, seasoned it, formed one larger and one smaller patty, then set them in the skillet to sizzle. Only when she returned to the fridge for lettuce, onion, mayo, mustard and tomato, did she realize Kell hadn't answered. She glanced over to find him staring, his expression caught between a frown and apprehension.

Uh-oh. "Kell?"

"Neither the car nor the suspect have been located, no." He turned his attention back to his laptop screen, but it was too late. There was something he didn't want her to know and she'd seen it there, the worry, the misgiving.

Double uh-oh. "But?"

Groaning his reluctance, he scrubbed his hands over his face before he pushed to his feet and came toward her, decision made. She found herself backing closer to the stove, bumping the skillet with her elbow.

"Watch it," Kell said, finding a spatula and flipping the meat while Jamie looked on.

What wasn't he telling her? "Kell, tell me."

"After lunch. Okay?"

Her stomach lurched, rattled. "Something's happened. What is it?"

"Nothing's happened. Not yet." He reached for a knife and the onion.

Meaning it was going to. And he knew it was going to. What had he done? And what hadn't he told her? She watched as he sliced the onion, dropping the rings into the grease from the burgers to brown.

Why not? What was a heart attack going to hurt when the killer caught up with her? She breathed deeply, searching for calm, finding a gnawing hunger instead. Her stomach growled. That didn't mean she was waiting till after lunch to find out what he was keeping from her.

"Kell? What do you think is going to happen? And when?"

Kell chuckled as he stirred the onions.

"What's so funny?"

"I am. Thinking you wouldn't want answers now. That you wouldn't figure out I had something up my sleeve."

"So? Talk," she said, using his knife to slice up half of the tomato, finding plastic wrap and storing the rest.

"You said something this morning about being able to see the killer coming—"

"He's coming here, isn't he?" The possibility slammed her so hard she almost doubled over. "To finish what he started ten years ago, right? And I'm not safe here at all."

Kell set down the spatula and placed his hands on her shoulders, then slid them up to cup her face "You're safe. One hundred percent safe. But I'm not so sure I am with the way you're gripping that knife."

What was he saying? A knife? God, oh, yes. God. "Sorry." Her hand shaking, she set it down on the counter. "I guess I was thinking I might need a weapon."

"Yeah. Saw that in your eyes." He let her go then, though reluctantly, as if not quite certain she was steady—she saw that in *his* eyes—then served up the burger patties onto paper towels to drain, and shut off the fire beneath.

She didn't care what he said. She wasn't going to wait until after lunch for the rest of the story. "Is he coming here or not, Kell? Tell me that much at least."

"If he does, we'll be ready for him," he told her staunchly.

That wasn't an answer. And what was this "we" business anyhow? "What are you talking about? How are you and I going to be ready when he took out four of my friends in the blink of an eye?"

And then she got it. By we, Kell wasn't talking about the two of them. "Who's going to be ready? Who else knows where we are? Does he know? Did he find out? Is that what you're not telling me?"

Kell had been loading plates with buns and meat and vegetables, and carrying them along with utensils and the squeeze bottles of mayonnaise and mustard to the table all the while Jamie had stood frozen. Now he took her by the hand and led her to eat.

Once they were seated, Kell continued. "This morning on the dock, you said something about being able to see him coming. It had me going back over all the precautions I'd taken in deciding to bring you here."

They'd driven back roads, a route that had taken twice as long as she assumed the trip normally took. Troopers had followed them to make sure no one else did. Even her mother had no idea where they were. But at least Jamie knew her mom was safe. She had her own set of bodyguards.

Jamie imagined Kell's contact person with the DPS knew; they'd have to stay in touch, after all. Or someone at the ranger station might need to know... Her eyes went wide and her whole chest tightened as she met Kell's gaze over the burger he'd lifted to bite.

"The leak," she said. "If there is a leak in your office, if that's how he found me in Weldon, then the killer knows where we are."

Kell shook his head, set down his burger and headed back to the kitchen for a roll of paper towels. Once he returned, he did his best to set her at ease. "Yes and no. Right now, Norm Greenley is the only one who knows where we are, though obviously, anyone with the capability and access can trace the GPS in my phone or the SUV."

This was not good. "Who has the capability and access?"

"For starters, the techs who monitor the various software programs."

Techs. Oh, God. "Like the one who recorded my hypnosis session?"

Kell nodded, bit into his burger again, chewed. "Megan Holly's only been in the office three years. She transferred in from the Georgia Bureau of Investigation. We're not ruling her out, but she's not the most likely suspect."

There was that royal "we" again. Jamie twisted her hands in her lap. "Who is the most likely? And who is 'we'?"

"Me and Greenley are the we. And as far as suspects,

there's a male tech, Hispanic, who's been in the department since 1995. He was born here, but has family in Mexico. In particular, a half brother who's been in and out of jail for petty offenses most of his life."

Oh God. "You found that out today?"

Kell nodded. "I phoned Greenley while you were showering. He took my theory and ran with it. Did a background check on Vargas when his jacket turned up the brother's sheet."

Fast work. "So you did what? Put out a warrant or APB or whatever on the brother?

"Not exactly," Kell said, filling his mouth with another huge bite that made talking impossible. As a delay tactic, it worked.

Frustrated, Jamie figured she might as well put her own burger together before the beef and sautéed onions got too cold to enjoy. If she had it in her to enjoy anything anymore, which she doubted. Still, she had a feeling she was going to need her strength.

"Then what exactly did you do?" she asked, using the last of the tomato slices, skipping the lettuce, and going light on the mayo and onions. Her stomach grumbled. The food really did smell good.

"Greenley had Vargas track my SUV," he said, completely matter-of-factly.

Jamie took a bite of her burger. She'd known where this was going since she'd first mentioned the leak. And once she'd recovered from the initial shock of fearing the killer was coming, she'd braced herself for the worst—that he was.

Of course, it had never occurred to her that Kell

would send him an engraved invitation, which seemed to be what he and Greenley had done. She tried not to sigh. Or scream. "Since the troopers followed us here, wouldn't Greenley's request raise a red flag? I mean, why would Greenley need the location of your SUV from Vargas when he knows where it is?"

"Vargas has no idea about the troopers. No reason he would, unless they told him. Since they're not based in Midland and most likely don't know him, there wouldn't be, so no red flag." Kell pushed away from the table and returned to the kitchen again, this time for two cans of soda.

"That still doesn't explain why Greenley would want your location when he knows exactly where you are," she said as Kell sat and scooted his chair back into place. She reached for her soda and popped the top, knowing she should trust him to do his job. But this was her life. She needed more than a pat on the head. "I can't see how his request wouldn't set off warning bells for Vargas, if he's really the leak."

His burger on his plate, his wrists against the table's edge, Kell leaned forward, his gaze catching hers and holding it tight. "What he's told Vargas is to watch for movement. We have no reason to go anywhere. So if the killer shows up and demands we drive to a more remote location, say, some out-of-the-way place like the spot he took Kass Duren, Vargas will be watching and know something's wrong."

And ostensibly report back to Greenley…or if he wanted to give his brother time to make his escape, maybe not. "What if the killer shows up and just shoots us in the head? Leaves the SUV where it is? Or makes us drive his car?"

"It's a ploy, sweetheart," Kell told her. "That's all. To make sure Vargas gives us up to his brother."

Okay, she was definitely not cut out for this cat-and-mouse stuff. "He won't know that?"

"No reason he should. He'll just think he's doing his job, following Greenley's orders. As long as he's been in the department, he'll understand Greenley's hedging against every move the suspect might make, no matter how far a reach."

It sounded reasonable, she supposed. Except… "You don't know for sure his brother is the killer. Or that Vargas is the leak."

"True," Kell said, sitting back. "That's why Greenley's going to surreptitiously see that word gets out. The fact that I have a cabin in the Guadalupes is common knowledge around the office. If Vargas isn't the leak, the information on our location will hopefully get back to whoever is."

"If there is a leak. If the killer hasn't just been watching me all this time."

He nodded, finishing off his food.

Jamie could only stare at hers. "Either way, we'll never know he's coming. No matter what I said about being able to see if he was."

"That's okay," Kell told her, the smile on his face deliciously, deviously wicked. "Because we're no longer the only ones watching. Greenley and his boys have got our back. There's no way anyone is getting to us without first going through them."

19

WITHOUT LOOKING at a clock, Kell knew it was after midnight. He also knew Jamie was pretending to sleep. The cabin only had one bed, meaning they shared it, or he slept on the couch. Since she hadn't made the suggestion when he'd joined her, he figured she'd come to terms with his plan. A good thing, since he needed her on board.

He never should have told her he'd set up the two of them as bait. Yes, she deserved to know, but it made this whole…thing—was it a relationship?—between them harder to deal with because he'd done it without telling her first.

Overhead, the cane ceiling fan stirred the air, squeaking in a maddening rhythm while drawing the heat from Kell's body. He needed a can of WD-40. He needed a second bedroom, or a longer, more comfortable sofa. He needed a way out of this mess that was guaranteed to save Jamie's life.

He'd done what his experience as a Texas Ranger dictated he do. If it had been anyone but Jamie, he wouldn't be caught up in this circle of second-guessing; every time he told himself he'd done the right thing, he came right back to feeling he'd done wrong by Jamie.

And those feelings were all tangled up with the ones he had for her. The ones making failure impossible. Sleep, too.

"I'm awake, you know."

He closed his eyes, swallowed, opened them again. "I know."

"You can talk to me if you have something on your mind," she said softly.

"I know." He left it at that, mostly because he didn't know what to say. He wasn't going to apologize for doing what he'd done. And if his job cost him her love…

Wow. Yeah. Best he leave it at that.

Jamie sighed, rolling onto her back. "I'm not mad at you."

Anger he could handle. Anger could be worked through. It was hatred he didn't want. Hatred meant she felt strongly, just not the things he wanted her to feel. "You've got to know, I would never put you in more danger. If I thought for a minute that he could get through us to you…"

"I want to be as confident as you are that he can't. That he won't." She pulled the sheet to her chin and held it there. "I'm just not that brave."

Not that brave? Kell found himself frowning, and turned onto his side, keeping the distance he was waiting for her to close. "This guy wasted no time in coming to you after the hypnosis and Duren's body was ID'd. If this goes down, it's going to happen fast. I've got men on every road, footpath, hiking and biking trail that lead to the cabin. He's not going to get to you. It's not going to happen."

"You're assuming he'll use a path or a road or a trail," Jamie countered. "He could be walking in as the crow flies even as we speak."

He could be, but Kell's men had more eyes and ears than their own. They had surveillance equipment. Heat sensors. Motion detectors. Parabolic mics. To avoid apprehension, the killer would have to slip in on a shadow, or like smoke. "He's not going to get to you."

She reached out with one hand and stroked it down the center of his chest. "The good guys don't always win, Kell."

"I will not let him get to you," he told her again, wondering for a moment which of them he was reassuring. He squeezed her fingers, held them over his fast-beating heart.

"I know you'll do your best—"

"No, sweetheart." He was not going to let her lie down and give up. Not after ten years spent in hiding. Not after he'd just found her. "Getting to you is going to require going through me. And I've got a really big gun."

She laughed softly. "That does make me feel better. Even if we're not talking about the same weapon."

His breath caught, his cock thickened. "It's all yours. Anytime, anywhere."

Her nails scratched lightly over his skin. "As long as it's not in my driveway, you mean."

"Next time we're there," he said and sucked back a sharp breath at her touch. "I promise."

"Promise me there will be a next time?" Her fingers were moving now, searching, surrounding. "That we'll get out of here in one piece?"

He would die making sure it happened. But rather than put the emotion overwhelming him into words that would sound too simple, he brought her face close and kissed her, speaking to her in the only way that felt right.

He knew about love. He'd grown up in a home where there was never a question that his parents would make up after fighting. Where actions spoke louder than words, but where the words themselves were never in short supply, and were used wisely, appropriately, used to solve as well as to soothe. Yeah, he knew about love.

He didn't know about this, about Jamie, precious, a gift, making his heart swell, ache, crave, making his body hard, splintering his focus. She was his case, but she was so much more, and he opened his mouth over hers and asked her to be his everything.

Her lips parted, her tongue tasted his. She wedged her body so far beneath him that his only move was to cover her. He did, and she opened her legs, hooking her heels in the small of his back, pressing her hands to his spine. She was supple, pliant, warm like wax, melting into him.

He needed a condom, but he didn't want to turn away. His erection lay pressed between them, pulsing. His mouth hadn't tasted enough of her yet, and he wanted this mating to last until they were both too exhausted to move. If might very well be their last time—a thought he pushed away before it caused him to suffer and soften.

Her fingers massaging up and down his back, Jamie tilted her hips, seeking him. He groaned, freeing himself long enough to hang over the edge of the bed and dig his wallet from the jeans he'd kicked out of last night.

Once he was sheathed, he entered her, no foreplay, no seduction, no romance.

Her sigh as she sank into the mattress was of satisfaction, of a gratitude that humbled him, of love. He had given her something she wanted, a something he was quite certain touched her in places his cock never would, though not for his lack of trying.

He rocked against her, not thrusting, not stroking, but a simple rhythmic motion of his lower body that kept them pressed together from belly to breast, as did his arms scooped beneath her. His head he rested beside hers on her pillow, sharing the air that she breathed.

Neither one of them said a word, they loved gently, slowly, though sounds of pleasure—gasps, moans, whimpers—were impossible to hold back, and punctuated the whir of the cane fan above.

And when neither of them could deny their bodies, they came together, the completion ripping into the core of his soul.

WHEN JAMIE FINALLY WOKE on her first day as killer bait, it was almost noon. Consumed by exhaustion, she'd never even heard Kell get out of bed, or smelled the scent of coffee that still lingered in the air. Neither had she heard him in the main room, walking in the kitchen, talking on his phone, though she was quite certain he had.

She pushed up to her elbows and listened. Then she sat up in the center of the bed. Still not a sound, prompting her to pull on the clothes she'd worn yesterday and left on the floor beside the bed. She'd shower after the mystery was solved. And, middle of nowhere or not, she had no idea whose eyes were prying. She was not going to walk outside in her skin.

Standing in the center of the front porch and shading her eyes, she found Kell sitting sideways in the driver's seat of his SUV, the door opened, his cell phone pressed to his ear. She didn't want to disturb him, but was curious what conversation had sent him outside to talk. They were too deeply involved in this game of catch a killer for secrets.

He saw her movements peripherally, turned toward her and gestured for her to come near. He smiled as he did it, and she relaxed. He didn't tell her to wait. He didn't hurriedly end the call. He welcomed her, and she was glad, even though what she heard told her nothing. He was responding in brief affirmatives, shaking his head as if it made a difference to the person on the other end of the sound waves. That made her smile, and he held out a hand, pulling her to stand between his thighs.

She leaned back against his chest with his arm around her, staring into the distance, wondering where the members of his team were posted, wondering if the killer was on his way. He kept her there until he'd finished, not even a minute, then he turned her and kissed her until she had to pull away to breathe.

"I've been waiting since dawn to do that."

"I seem to remember you doing the same thing not long before. Did you sleep at all?"

"I never sleep when a case is coming down to the wire. I've got too much going on in my mind. It's insomnia's fertile ground."

She wondered if their involvement made his insomnia worse. "Anything new since last night?"

A single nod. "Everyone's in place. Now we wait."

That would have to do. "And you're making your phone calls out here why?"

"Because that's what a prince does for his Sleeping Beauty," he told her, reaching up to tuck her hair behind her ear.

He made her want to laugh. He made her want to cry. He made her want to have his babies…and that was her clue to stop with the wanting. "And what is the prince planning to do about feeding me?"

He canted his head to the side and considered her. "How 'bout a picnic and a swim?"

"Should I paint a target on my back with ketchup?" she asked, considering him in return.

He gave her a look, then hopped down and closed up his SUV. Hooking his arm around her neck, he led her back to the cabin, saying, "I don't want to make you a target. I do want you to relax. That's all."

"In that case, I accept." She'd never had a man pamper her, and as much as she was enjoying Kell doing so, she reminded herself that this was nothing but a detour before she reached the city limits of Singletown where she'd be living the rest of her life. "You want me to do sandwiches?"

"Nope. I want you to change and go." He dropped a kiss on her forehead, then sent her on her way with a slap on her ass. "I'll meet you at the pond in a few."

It was a caveman gesture, and it had her smiling as she found her still-damp underwear and worked them on, then left through the back door, slapping him on his ass as she did. She fairly skipped down the dock to the pond, kicking off her sneakers and leaping into the water.

She surfaced, sputtering, the fright forgotten, the fun all she knew. Kell had done this for her, too. Given her back the parts of her life she'd hidden, out of sight, out of mind. For so long she'd felt she didn't deserve to know joy. That she needed to suffer for the families of the victims. Now she wanted to be happy, and she wanted Kell, forever.

"Stop it. Right now," she ordered herself. She could not keep doing this. Whatever happened, happened. And nothing was going to happen until she knew that for both of them, this relationship was built on more than her case.

"Hey you! Come and get it."

At the sound of Kell's voice, she turned where she was treading water, and swam back to the dock. When she got there, he was waiting, the box of food he'd carried down to the pond sitting next to her shoes. She took his hand when he offered it, tumbling against him when he tugged.

His bare chest was warm, his heart thumping, but her stomach won out. She pushed away and went for the sandwiches he'd stacked in the box between folded paper towels. He'd forgotten to bring drinks, but he had brought a knife—the one she'd gripped so hard in the kitchen yesterday.

She held it up for him to see. "Are you trying to tell me something?"

"Just thought it might make you feel better," he said, grabbing a sandwich and biting a quarter of it away.

She glanced down at the front of his board shorts, unable to help herself. "Because your gun's all out of ammo?"

"If it is, it's all your fault," he said, still chewing.

"I will gladly take the blame. As long as you trot yourself back to the cabin for drinks."

He mock frowned. "Trot? Is that princess for 'please'?"

Really, he was too cute for his own good. Or for hers. "Will you please get the drinks? And sunscreen?"

"As you wish," he said with a wink. "Just watch where you wave that thing. It's called a weapon for a reason."

She dropped to sit on the dock and watched him go, picnicking with herself while she waited for him to return. Oh, but she really could get used to this.

Yes, Weldon was small and quiet, but this…this was peaceful, serene. As if here time meant nothing—a thought that brought a second that was related.

Kell had been gone way too long.

She turned to look at the cabin, saw…nothing. Her sandwich-filled stomach tensed. He could've taken a phone call, but wouldn't he have walked down to the dock while doing so? He should've been back with their drinks by now.

Maybe she was borrowing trouble, overreacting, being plain ridiculous, but she could think of only one reason he wasn't. She got to her feet, slipped on and tied her shoes.

And then she picked up the knife.

20

REMINDING HIMSELF TO GRAB his phone that he'd forgotten to bring with the picnic, Kell frowned into the fridge, trying to remember what it was he wanted. Drinks, right. And, yeah. No matter what he'd told Jamie about his adrenaline-fueled insomnia, he needed sleep.

His sharp edge was dulled, his straight thinking meandering. How else could he explain staring at the cans of cold soda this long? As if they were going to jump into his hands. And now he was hearing things. He really he had to shake off this daze—

Whack!

The refrigerator door slammed him sideways. He stumbled, grabbed the counter for balance, bit off a succinct "What the hell?" and looked up.

Then he bit his tongue and watched the Hispanic man standing there use the hand with the snake tattoo to shut the fridge. His other hand held a gun. Kell did not like being on this end of it.

"The girl," the man—he was gangly, edgy, no more than five foot seven—said in accented English. "Down at the water. Get her to come here. Now."

Think, think, think. Kell remained silent, his sluggish

mind racing, his blood firing in his veins. The man knew where Jamie was, that she was there alone, yet had come after Kell instead. He obviously wanted Kell out of the way before taking care of Jamie. Otherwise, why not shoot her, dump her body in the water and go?

He didn't plan to go. He didn't want a quick kill. That was the only conclusion Kell could come to for the delay. And then he came to another, equally horrifying. Soon enough, this man would figure out that Jamie would eventually return to the cabin on her own. He did not need Kell to get her here. He didn't need Kell for anything.

That meant Kell had to find a reason to become indispensable before the man with the snake tattoo dispensed with him.

"She won't be able to hear me if I yell." It was a lie, of course. With only the whistling wind for noise, Jamie would hear him just fine.

But there was a glassiness to the other man's eyes that made Kell go for it, a stall tactic while he tried to figure out how his team had let this one through. Something was off, wrong. Something big. "And if I'm not back in another minute, she knows to run."

The Hispanic man's gaze sharpened, his thick black brows coming down in a vee. "There is no place for her to go. No one to help her."

Kell weighed how much of the truth to reveal. "I have a man—"

"You had a man. He is not there now."

He'd taken out one of the team. Goddammit. Kell didn't have time to wonder who, what had happened, how serious it was. He only had time for Jamie. "I have more. And once they realize one of their own has gone silent, they'll be coming here to get you."

"Then I will kill the girl, and you will be my hostage." The man raised his gun hand, wiping his sleeve beneath his nose. "Then when I am safely away, I will kill you."

A plan that would keep Kell alive for the moment. Now to work on keeping Jamie the same. He kept his hands where the other man could see them and took him in, the ragged athletic shoes, the worn jeans, dirty with torn hems, the long-sleeved plaid shirt that said hand-me-down charity. The glassy eyes, the runny nose…

"What were you after? At the Sonora Nites Diner? Money to fund your habit?"

He rolled his head on his shoulders, looked around the kitchen, came back on Kell with a wave of the gun. "The girl. Make her come here. Before she runs."

Kell started to tell him to go ahead, pull the trigger, but he wasn't certain that if Jamie heard the gunshot, she wouldn't run toward it instead of away. And with Kell down—or dead—he wouldn't be able to fulfill his promise to Dr. Kate that he'd bring her daughter home. Hell, he'd promised Jamie just last night that they'd get out of here in one piece.

In his line of work, he shouldn't be making promises.

C'mon, Kell, focus, think, focus. His gun was in the bedroom, his phone on the table, but Jamie had a knife…

"I'll have to walk to the dock, wave her up from there."

He was getting nervous, the tattooed man. He couldn't kill Kell and go after Jamie alone; he'd have no hostage should he get caught. And now that he'd revealed himself, he couldn't get to Jamie without going through Kell, and whatever he was on had him just paranoid enough not to go along with Kell's suggestion.

Kell was looking for his next move when he saw a shadow cross the wall behind the killer. He hadn't heard tires on the crushed-shell driveway or the rumble of an engine approaching—meaning the body creeping closer had to be Jamie's.

He kept his gaze trained on the man who held the gun, fought the rising fear that sent his heart to his throat to choke him, wished he had a better weapon than the only thing he'd seen within reach—the iron skillet he'd left on the stove top last night after washing it.

He backed a step closer to the door, closer to the skillet, too, praying that Jamie could hear him and that the killer couldn't hear her. "Is that what you want to do then? Have me wave her up from the dock? I can't say she won't run if she sees you've got a gun. Or sees that you're here, for that matter. Best bet is to let me walk down there alone. You'll still be able to see me, but she won't see you."

He was rambling now, but he wanted Jamie to come near enough without giving herself away, and leave him the knife on the table. That's what he assumed she intended to do, so when she rounded the corner with her arms over her head, all he could do was yell, "No!"

The killer turned. Jamie slammed the rock she held into the side of his skull, sending him spinning. Kell whipped the skillet off the stove and caught the man's flailing gun hand. The weapon skittered toward the back door. He stopped it with his foot, grabbed it up and straddled the man who was on the floor, holding his head in his hands.

"The bedroom. My service weapon," he said without looking at Jamie. She ran off, was back in seconds, still in her underwear and dripping pond water all over the floor. He reached over and released the safety. "Keep it pointed at his head. Shoot him if he moves."

Kell kept one eye on the man while scrounging through the kitchen's supply closet for something…rope, twine, a bungee cord, fishing line… Yes! Duct tape!

Yanking a strip from the roll, he nudged Jamie out of the way and bent at the man's feet to bind them. Next, he pulled his arms behind his back and did the same with his wrists. After that, he took the gun from Jamie and set the two safetied weapons on the table along with the roll of tape.

Finally, he braced his hands on his knees and leaned over to catch his breath. He was halfway through his recovery when he noticed her feet. "Where are your shoes?"

She curled the toes of one foot over those of the other. "Outside the bedroom window."

The window. Of course. He hadn't stopped long enough to think about how she'd gotten in. He straightened, his chest still tight and aching. "I leave you a knife and you come armed with a rock?"

Just as breathless as he was, she looked over her shoulder toward the bedroom, then looked back at him. "I brought the knife. I left it on the windowsill. I figured I stood a better chance against a rock if he turned it on me."

Smart cookie. But just for the record…and because

he wouldn't be able to live with himself if he lost her while she was trying to save him… "Promise me you'll never do anything like that again."

"The way it looks, I won't have to," she said softly, her voice breaking at the end.

He followed the direction of her gaze; when he looked back, he found her shaking, crying, on the verge of collapse. Cursing himself for a jerk, he grabbed her against him so fast he knocked away what breath he'd managed to catch. He didn't care, not about anything but taking care of her.

It was over. The terror of her last ten years. No, he didn't have the answers to explain what had happened today, or what had happened at the Sonora Nites Diner. Not yet. But he would have them soon. All of them. That was his job.

Jamie, she was his life. "No, sweetheart. You won't have to. Not ever again."

"I LOVE YOU, SWEETIE. And I am so happy to be waking up from this nightmare. I'll see you when you get here."

"I love you, too, Mom. And so am I. Bye-bye." Jamie ended the call with her mother, then handed the phone back to Kell who sat beside her on the top of the cabin's front steps.

"I'll bet Kate's relieved," he said. He had already made all the calls he needed to hours ago, checking in with his team, seeing to the officer who'd been shot, calling for whoever it was that would take the killer away.

Jamie had waited for all of that to be done before phoning her mother. She'd wanted to be able to deliver the good news that the ordeal was now behind them, the killer off the street and out of their lives.

"Yes. Very." Jamie nodded, strangely nervous. She'd finished with her mother, and the members of law enforcement who'd been here were gone.

It was just them now. Her and her Texas Ranger. The two of them alone, safe, the baggage of the last ten years lighter, and less of a stumbling block between them. She was still having trouble breathing, however, not to mention believing the events of the previous eight hours.

Once the suspect had been contained and she'd recovered her composure, dried her skin and her tears, and changed out of her wet clothes, Kell had left her holding his gun long enough to retrieve rope from his SUV's toolbox and reinforce the job he'd done with the duct tape.

Then he'd taken her out to the front porch while he'd contacted Greenley and the rest. She'd been out here ever since, sitting on the steps, or in one of the porch rockers, or for a while on the porch itself. She hadn't gone back into the cabin except once to use the restroom. She'd watched the comings and goings of the authorities from whichever vantage point kept her out of their way.

While she and Kell had waited for them to arrive— a long wait considering his cabin's location—Kell had made more sandwiches, leaving the ones on the dock for the birds who'd discovered the feast not long after Jamie had abandoned it, swimming to the other side of the pond and trekking the long way through the brush to the cabin in search of Kell.

It was when she'd reached the open bedroom window

that she'd decided she didn't trust herself with the knife she'd brought with her. She was scared, feared she'd be too physically shaken to hold on and would lose it in a fight. She'd seen the rock, and been much less intimidated by the thought of using it as a weapon.

She'd hoped she wouldn't need a weapon at all. She'd hoped she'd find Kell had fallen and twisted his ankle, or for some reason was sick on the bathroom floor. What she'd found had been worse than any of her imaginings—the man who had killed her friends, threatening to take her lover's life.

She shuddered now, reminding herself that she'd gotten through that horrible moment—and those that followed—just as she had through the last ten years, though this time she'd had more of a reason to do so, one more valuable than staying alive. She'd had to make sure Kell survived, that he did not sacrifice his life for hers.

Sitting beside her, his forearms on his knees, Kell clutched the phone with both hands, squinting as he stared into the distance, his mouth grim. Jamie loved the crow's feet that stepped from his eyes to his temples.

She did not like the tense set of his jaw, and laid a hand on his thigh to tell him. "It's the end of a case, not the end of the world. You'll get more chances to wear your white hat and be a hero."

He dropped his head forward, a grin teasing at his lips. "After these last few days, I'm pretty much considering taking early retirement."

She knew he was kidding, but she liked a lot the idea of him never again facing the wrong end of a gun. She also liked seeing him smile. It helped with the scary part of not knowing what came next. "And let the bad guys win? I don't think so."

"There are plenty of candidates itching for this job. The bad guys don't stand a chance." He reached for her hand, laced their fingers, squeezed. "But then sometimes the good guys don't either."

"Oh, Kell," she said, pulling free to wrap her arms around him, to pillow her head on his shoulder and hold him close, staring out over his property at the safe world beyond. And it was safe now. She just knew it. "I'm so sorry about your man. But he should be okay, yes?"

"Yeah, as long as he comes through surgery. It's something we all face. That possibility, taking a bullet." He patted her arm where it lay across his chest, tilted his head to rest against hers. "But thank you. For understanding. For being here."

She loved him. "Where else would I be?"

"Yeah. About that." He sighed, made as if to move away, to stand, but only got as far as pulling his feet to the step beneath the one where they sat, remaining in the circle of her arms. "I guess we'd better pack up and get you back to Weldon. Before it gets any later."

She took a deep breath. Here went nothing. Unless it was everything. And if she didn't go for it, she would never know. "Or we could not pack."

He looked over, his expression broadcasting his confusion. "You don't want to pack?"

"I don't want to go back to Weldon." She let her arms fall away from him, and knitted her hands in her lap. Never before had she felt such a need to be brave. "Not yet."

"You want to stay here?" he asked after a short, cautious pause.

She nodded, treading carefully, too. "I'm thinking, it's been ten years. I deserve a true vacation. It would be my first."

Another pause. "And you want to take it here?"

"I do." Deep breath, deep breath. "But it would be nice not to take it alone."

"Me?" It was all he asked, his voice soft, his tone wary as if he were walking a razor's edge of hope.

Hope she could give him. "Of course you. Who else?"

"I don't know." He stretched, but the tension remained, radiating toward her. "I thought maybe your mother."

Now, *that* was funny. "I love my mother. I would never have gotten through the last ten years without her. But I've seen her every day of them. And if I were to take a vacation with her, it would be a cruise, or to a spa. She and I and isolation wouldn't mix."

"But you like being isolated with me."

"I love being isolated with you. And before you run away scared because I used the L word—"

He turned toward her, his eyes flashing, hot and proud and suddenly supremely confident. "Use it again."

Gulp. "What?"

"Use it again," he demanded, pressing, intense. Potent as he growled. "Or else I'm going to."

Oh my. Oh my. This was real. She could barely find her voice. "Then you go first."

"I love you, Jamie," he said, cupping her nape and threading his fingers through her hair. "I know it's been less than a week. I know this has been a wild trial by fire. But I would love you if I'd brought my kid into your clinic for an appointment and met you there."

"You have a kid?" she asked, a question as crazy as what was happening here.

"Not yet. That would be getting ahead of ourselves, don't you think?" he asked, one wicked brow rising. "Unless I'm reading you wrong."

She shook her head, shook it again, kept shaking it until the words and the tears shook free, and her hair began to tumble. "You're not. I love you Kell. It's been fast and furious. A whirlwind. But it would've been just the same if we hadn't spent our first week together catching a killer."

"It'll be the only week we spend doing anything like that," he promised, hefting her up to straddle his thighs.

She looped her arms around his neck, her vision blurred, her heart a swollen mess of emotions. "So we can stay here for a while?"

"What about your job?" he asked.

As if she cared. The only thing she cared about was this. Him. Her Texas Ranger. Her Kell. "Six years of accrued vacation, remember? And then I may just take leave. Or quit."

Half-moon dimples appeared beneath the scruff covering his face. "All these life changes. Maybe you'd also consider moving? Somewhere not too far from your mother?"

"My mother would have no trouble sending me packing if she knew I was happy."

This time his gaze softened, grew dreamy, and just a little bit damp. "Are you happy, Jamie?"

"Exquisitely," she told him before he brought her mouth to his and kissed her with all he had. How could she be anything but in the arms of her one good man?

We'll be spotlighting a different series
every month throughout 2009
to celebrate our 60th anniversary.

Look for Silhouette® Nocturne™ in October!

Travel through time to experience tales
that reach the boundaries of life and death.
Bestselling authors Lindsay McKenna, Cindy
Dees, P.C. Cast and Merline Lovelace join
together in a brand-new, four-book
Time Raiders miniseries.

TIME RAIDERS

August—*The Seeker*
by *USA TODAY* bestselling author Lindsay McKenna

September—*The Slayer* by Cindy Dees

October—*The Avenger*
by *New York Times* bestselling author and
coauthor of the House of Night novels P.C. Cast

November—*The Protector*
by *USA TODAY* bestselling author Merline Lovelace

Available wherever books are sold.